THUNDEROUS AP1

MW00986400

"Dara Joy . . . sets our hearts ablaze with a romance of incandescent brilliance. An electrifying talent, Ms. Joy delivers a knockout love story in which the romance is red hot and the adventure out of this world. In a word, wow!"
-Romantic Times (Rejar)

"Hotter than a firecracker on the 4th of July, this fiery gem of a love story is another spectacular landmark in the shooting star career of one of the romance genre's most fabulous talents."
-Romantic Times (Mine To Take)

"An author who skillfully hides sub-text under inventive storytelling is, to me, a highly talented author, and I doff my hat to the Joys of the world who manage to do this. Her stories have a staying power that is incredible and every single time I go back to one of them, I find something new that jumps out at me. This is multi-layered."
-All About Romance

"RITUAL OF PROOF is an engaging Regency romantic fantasy that turns the classic roles of the Ton totally around and upside down in a wonderful role reversal. The amusing story line, reminiscent of Travolta's 'White Man's Burden' but with humor, is fun due to the gender bending and the use of puns on accepted vernacular. Dara Joy lives

up to her surname as she provides an entertaining satirical tale that cries for more novels on this reverse Regency world."
-Harriet Klausner for Allreaders.com

"Dara Joy is a remarkable and unique talent... She is definitely an author to watch."
-ReadersRead.com

"Page for page it was the most original, enjoyable novel I've read in months, maybe years."
-Susan Scribner Theromanacereader.com (Rejar)

"This book is every other writer's nightmare. It is well written, no sagging middle, no big misunderstanding plot, no 'I hate you, Milord, and hope you get quartered and burned at the stakes' lines. It has no lingering descriptions of everything or prolonged psycho-analytical conversations a character has with himself. The dialogue is quick and to the point. The story is utterly funny and serious. The sex is. . . well. . .inventive, to say the least, definitely an NC-17, not at all rude, just sensual to its utmost degree."
- All About Romance (Reviewer Liana LaRiccia for Rejar Desert Isle Keeper)

"After putting in a special order in December, just got, and devoured in 1 gulp, this book of Ms. Joy's. The lovemaking was so passionate, yet unbelievably tender, so heart

meltingly loving... I think if they ever knew about this book, all men would try and get the book banned, 'cos the hero is perfect, and he would set the bar so high, no mortal male could even come close."
-Writerspace.com (MTT)

"There is a rising star in the genre who absolutely does not write books that are similar to any others and that is Dara Joy, an author who [was] literally an overnight success..."
-The Romance Reader

"The bright, shining star of fabulous new author Dara Joy gains added luster with this scintillating romance. . . . Sparkling with intelligence and wit to please the most discriminating of readers. A joy indeed!"
-Romantic Times, Review of High Energy

"The characters' consciousness insidiously slips into your own and takes you far beyond any expectations. Thank you Dara for the strength you give your characters, for their enigmatic nature so full of magic, for the purpose you give their actions,and for the subtle meanings you contribute to our lives."
-Likesbooks.com/ reviewed by Liana La Ricia (MTT - Desert Isle Keeper)

"Dara Joy . . . writes with a wit, warmth and intelligence that will have readers flocking. . . . A full-bodied love

story brimming with fiery sensuality and emotional intensity."
-Romantic Times, Review of Knight of a Trillion Star

"Readers will be delighted with this fantasy/space travel romance."
-Affaire de Coeur, Review of Knight of a Trillion Star

". . . A delightful romp of a romance where old-fashioned sex can be fun. *Tonight or Never* is destined to garner {Ms. Joy} new fans."
-Romantic Times (Tonight or Never)

"Hip, Hip, Hooray! Dara Joy has done it again! This author has one of the truly inventive and devious minds in the romantic field. This book is a sterling example."
-The Ridiculous Book Store

"All in all I would say this book was just about purrfect."
-http://louisabrown.net

"Dara Joy proves herself a master at both erotic and comedic writing. She has created one of the funniest books I have ever read."
 -epinions.com (TON)

"This NY TIMES best-selling author writes in a unique voice!"
-RomanticTimes

"If you love great stories with great characters you're going to love Dara Joy."
- Jen's PLace

This is a work of fiction. Names, characters, places, and incidents are products of the author's imagination or are used fictitiously and are not to be construed as real. Any resemblance to actual events, locales, organizations, or persons, living or dead, is entirely coincidental.

Copyright 2004 Dara Joy
ISBN: 0-9753549-0-6

All rights reserved. No part of this book may be used or reproduced in any manner whatsoever without written permission, except in the case of brief quotations embodied in critical articles and reviews. For information address House of Sages at INFO@OFFICIALDARAJOY.COM

House of Sages tradesize paperback July 2004 FIRST PRINTING, FIRST EDITION.

Visit Dara Joy on the World Wide Web at WWW.OFFICIALDARAJOY.COM

Printed in United States of America

To my wonderful readers,

If you are holding this book in your hand it means that you love my work. You are willing to stand up for it, regardless of format. So, in other words, I am speaking to family. As most of you know this book was produced under unusual circumstances. There are no words to truly tell you what your purchase of this book means to me except to say thank you for making me get up every day with the desire to write for you. I have the best readers in this and any universe.

I also want to tip my vintage hat to the countless booksellers and librarians, worldwide, who contacted me and asked to help me in my endeavors to get this work out. These people work tirelessly, making sure that all of us are able to read the books of our choice. They work long hours with little compensation, just to keep our written "worlds" alive. They have my utmost respect, admiration, and gratitude– not just as a writer, but as a reader, as well.

At the time this book was originally being prepared to go to press my father tragically suffered a fall in the bathtub. He was in intensive care for several days but sadly succumbed to his injuries and passed away. I was unable to do a final copyedit of the work and I hope you will forgive me any minor mistakes in punctuation etc., that may have slipped under the radar. I felt that it was more important to get the book out to you; rather than postpone the print lineup.

For those of you who collect books, this is sure to be a unique item!

I hope that these heartfelt stories will speak to you the way they spoke to me.

This book is dedicated to all who love the written word, who support the creative mind, and who travel the road of the heart.

Love,
Dara

p.s. Welcome home.

Revoked but not yet canceled
The gift goes on
In silence
In a bell jar
Still a song ...
You've got to shake your fists at lightning now
You've got to roar like forest fire
You've got to spread your light like blazes
All across the sky
They're going to aim the hoses on you
Show 'em you won't expire
Not till you burn up every passion

                    -Joni Mitchell, Judgement of
                    the Moon and Stars

Table of Contents

THAT FAMILIAR TOUCH

Those who will play with cats must expect to get scratched.

-Miguel de Cervantes

Planet M'yan, Familiar homeworld, 5187 m.u.

"He cannot stop me from leaving!"

Soosha was so angry she could feel the hair on the back of her head lifting. The signal usually was a warning that a full-scale battle was on its way. "Who is he to tell me what to do?"

"*He* is the King of All Familiar." H'riar sighed deeply. It was a weary, drawn-out exhalation. This was the fifth time he had had this 'discussion' with his brother's daughter!

On occasion, the girl could be as stubborn as her older brother, Brygar.

Unfortunately, this was such an occasion.

He sighed again, shaking his head.

H'riar had always thought Soosha the sweetest and prettiest of his family's kits, with her smoky black hair, aqua/gold eyes, engagingly inquisitive features and happy disposition. Normally she was the most even tempered among the entire family.

Except when her fur was rubbed the wrong way.

Then, beware!

"Yes, Soosha, he *can* stop you." H'riar reiterated that for the eleventh time.

The Familiar girl began to pace. Another bad sign.

"He is being unreasonable! I will be perfectly fine."

"Taj Gian disagrees." Recently, their king had recalled all Familiar back to their homeworld of M'yan, forbidding any off-planet travel.

Even trips to Aviara were curtailed.

Of course, he had done this for their safety. Karpon, the despotic ruler of Ganakari, had declared an all out war on the Familiar. He was systematically hunting them down and enslaving them.

Unfortunately, their people were considered by most to be a beautiful and sensual species– thus they brought very high prices on the auction block. Their extraordinary abilities in the art of pleasure-giving had seen to that.

H'riar knew that his people's gift of shapeshifting made them endlessly fascinating to others; for Familiar walked in two forms– that of man and cat.

But with this innate ability also came a vital sense of individuality.

His People refused to be contained or controlled. Regardless of the source.

Thus H'riar's current dilemma.

It had not set well with the King to issue such a proclamation. Yet taj Gian knew that, above all, he had to protect his people.

At first H'riar had not been sure about the course of action Gian was determined to take, but as the King's advisor, or *utal*, he came to understand and agree with Gian's decision.

Soosha did not see it the same way.

As a strong-willed female coming into her prime, she had other ideas. Being related to a king sometimes had its advantages. Soosha was under the erroneous impression that taj Gian's decree could not possibly include her.

H'riar, like every other male member of the family, had always been charmed by her beguiling ways. The fact that she was the youngest female in the family simply added to the winsome equation.

In other words, she was used to getting her way.

H'riar tried once more to make her understand.

"He is not being unreasonable, Soosha; he is trying to protect our people."

"Do you think someone will get the better of me? I can take care of myself, I assure you!" Her nostrils flared in a charming display of feline temperament.

H'riar tried not to smile. She was young and inexperienced in the ways of other worlds. Her bravado came from untried youth.

But it would not do to tell her that.

Soothing was by far the best tactic with an outraged Familiar woman. That is, unless your intention was to rile one up– which was always interesting under the right circumstances.

He smiled fondly at a memory of just such an incident with his own mate. . . .

Soosha's howl of outrage snapped him back to the present.

"I have come of age! It is my time to travel on adventures,

H'riar. I have waited my whole life for this! It is unreasonable!"

To be fair, she was not the only one to have such sentiments. Many of their youth were tugging at the restrictions taj Gian had been forced to place on all of them. Although the people understood his reasoning and accepted it, the closing of the secret Tunnel on M'yan had been difficult for everyone.

They were a people who lived for adventure. No Familiar could stand a cage– even a cage as vast as an entire planet. Truly, it was the *idea* of being told 'not to' that made them 'want to' all the more.

This was the nature of any cat.

H'riar acknowledged to himself that they often were an infuriating, yet engaging people.

"I am deeply sorry that your coming of age has to be so confined. Yes, you will not be able to experience all that others have in the past, but, Soosha, there are things off world of which you have no comprehension. Terrible things. Your safety is too important to us. Please understand."

Now it was Soosha's turn to sigh. "Please try to understand *me*, H'riar; this is not simply a coming of age whim to adventure. My whole life I have dreamt of exploring other worlds! Other beings. I want to see how others live. How they think. I know it is unusual for a woman to want to go adventuring so afar, but I am not afraid to take this chance in order to experience new things. I should be allowed to decide for myself!"

H'riar rubbed his forehead. How could he get through to her? She would not be able to understand the depths of cruelty she could encounter. On M'yan she had known only love and compassion. Male familiars were very protective of their mates and families. And for good reason. The universe was an especially dangerous place for them.

"Most of these beings you wish to meet do not think as we do; they not share our beliefs or even care about them. Did you know that in the Far Reaches there are beings who survive solely by dealing in the trading of captive beings? Familiars are highly prized by them."

Soosha paled but held her ground. "I have heard of this, H'riar. But it is males they seek. I would not be in danger."

"It is males they seek because they have not easily encountered any of our females. Would you risk being captured and sold like a piece of krilli cloth? Forced to do things so horrible you cannot even imagine?"

Soosha swallowed. Such a fate held little appeal. Still, she could not give up her dream.

"That would not happen to me. Furthermore, if our males are willing to take such a risk to adventure then I should be allowed to do the same. Besides, it is uncommon for Familiars to be taken. Our men have a way of escaping, do they not?"

"That has been changing. Furthermore, you know that the Familiar male is a born predator, Soosha. He has ways of protecting himself that you do not."

That gave her pause. While their females had some predator in them, they were not like the males in that regard. A cornered male was a sight to behold! If he was in the right mood, he would stand his ground and fight no matter how many he faced.

Still, females could often outthink their enemies; she was not about to give up her lifelong dream.

"What you say may be true, H'riar, but I have different

ways. Ways that are stronger – in some areas – than a male's."

Do we men not know that! H'riar could not decide whether to smile at the charming girl or frown at her stubbornness.

"Nonetheless, my little Soosha, this discussion is pointless. Your brother would never agree to it and Taj Gian has sealed the Tunnel. He has commanded us *all* to remain planetside. You will not be going anywhere until the situation on Ganakari is cleared and their leader Karpon has answered for his crimes against us."

"But that could take years!" The girl wailed.

"So it could. Thus you will have plenty of time to enjoy your native land. Perhaps you will even mate?"

Her lip stuck out mutinously. "I will not mate before I adventure!"

"You are too young to realize that mating can be an adventure in itself." He winked at her. "I must get back to the royal abode, Soosha. I hope my visit has soothed your anxiety. Now that you understand that your wish to travel is impossible, perhaps you would like to come to the palace in a few days for a visit? Jenise would appreciate your company and Gian will not stop the men from showering you in gifts."

Soosha nostrils flared slightly at the innocuous suggestion, but she wished H'riar a good day and thanked him for coming.

Discussion over, the *utal* quickly took his leave.

Soosha plopped onto the nearest floor cushion.

H'riar actually thinks he can pet me into compliance! She snorted delicately as she stretched across the silken fabric. *Come to the palace!* What did she care of gifts from hopeful, vying males?

The whole thing bored her. And while she was very fond of the *tajan*, Jenise, she did not wish to wile away her time in the royal abode. She had exploring to do– and she was going to do it!

But how?

She bit her lip.

Since Gian had sealed the secret Tunnel, the only other Tunnel on M'yan led directly to Aviara. That Tunnel was heavily guarded on both sides: the Charl knights protected the entrance on the Aviaran side, and the clans rotated their best men to guard the entrance on M'yan.

No one was allowed through without official approval.

Hmm. Unlike the secret Tunnel that had been sealed, the other Tunnel connected to the great Hall of Tunnels on Aviara. . . .

Although she did not want to be on Aviara, perhaps she might be able to slip away once inside the vast Hall of Tunnels and from there link to another world?

Once she was off Aviara, her journey would be assured. She need only take additional Tunnel jumps from that point.

Of course, it would be best to hide her course by going through several Tunnels so she could not be easily tracked.

It might actually work, she reasoned.

But how could she get to Aviara without official permission? Would there be a way to get through the Tunnel gate undetected?

She didn't know, but she was going to find out.

Running up to her chambers, she quickly grabbed a pouch of clarified stones and one of her colorful sashes. She tucked the stones into a secret pocket hidden within the waistband, before wrapping the band around her waist.

Then she twirled a green hooded cloak over her loose *jatal-riaz*. The flowing, filmy material of the *jatal-riaz* had been expertly wrapped around her thirty-nine times, then tied off in the traditional way. The cool krilli cloth draped her body, moving as sensuously as she did. Just the feel of the silken fabric rubbing against her skin made her purr.

Familiar males would often stop whatever they were doing just to watch the beautiful, graceful vision of a woman as she passed by in her *jatal-riaz*.

The simple green cloak was nowhere near as extravagant as the other ones she had and it made her sad to have to wear it on such a momentous occasion; but its plain lines would not draw extra attention to her.

Soosha gave a little mournful mew. Like most Familiar, she loved to preen in beautiful things; however, hidden beneath this traveler's cloak, she would easily be mistaken for a member of a trading caravan.

As long as she did not look anyone directly in the eye.

The distinctive dual-colored eyes of her kind would immediately give her away– so she would have to be very careful.

Soosha stuck her head out the door to make sure no one was about to witness her slip away. Her eyes widened at the sight of a very old man walking up the hill to their family home. He was leaning heavily on a wizard's staff.

Yaniff.

What was that old Charl doing here? And why had he chosen this of all times to visit?!

The seventh level mystic would know in an instant what she was planning! She twitched her ears. What should she

24

do. . . . !

She held her breath as Yaniff suddenly veered from the path he had been following and changed direction to head towards the royal abode.

Soosha let out a huge sigh of relief.

He must have been looking for H'riar and realized that the King's advisor was already on his way back to Gian.

Now that the path was clear, she quickly dashed out of the house and into the shelter of the surrounding vegetation.

A satisfied smile licked her lips.

Nothing was so delightful as darting out of a door as if someone might stop you at any given moment. Soosha was not sure why that felt so good– *it just did.*

With a happy laugh she swatted some leaves on the branch of a bush as she sprinted past.

Taking a shortcut through the dense foliage would help her avoid running into anyone; although Familiars did not have a tendency to stick to pathways. Especially if they could get into mischief along an alternate route.

Her people were known to spend hours happily engaged in intense distraction. After all, who knew what interesting things one might find along any journey?

Today, Soosha forced herself to remain focused on her goal. The flowers around the lagoon would not distract her. Today, she was the hunter!

And the portal near the royal abode was her quarry.

Very soon her new journeys would begin.

They had been calling her.

Calling. . .

Planet Spoltam, ruling city of Aghni

Daxan Sahain viewed the city before him from the comfort and strength of his white stone balcony.

The lofty plateau effectively delineated him as a sophisticated member of the ruling class of Spoltam.

He slowly raised his face to the sky.

The bright sunlight– a constant daily event in this city– glinted off white marble roofs, stone pillars, and towering porticos. The warming rays skipped across the crystal clear turquoise waters of the bay of Aghni like a Spoltam signal torch shining a lighted path to the beauty of their city.

At night, moonlight did much the same; but instead of gold, silver shimmered on the city streets.

Thus, day and night, the city appeared as a glittering jewel perched high on the edge of the Prionian Sea.

Centuries ago, it had been designed by their best

architects to be the privileged nexus of Spoltam.

Below him, on the streets, citizens and travelers alike bustled through the market stalls, shops, and plazas. Some busily haggling for items. Others gossiping over the finest imported libations.

In this city, almost every luxury in the known universe could be had– for a price. It was a good place to live if you were the *right* kind of Spoltam citizen.

For himself, Daxan enjoyed a very fine life in Aghni.

His large home, replete with servants who were ready to do his bidding, day or night, testified to his eminent place in society. His table was always full, his bed never empty.

As a scholar, he was afforded the most pleasurable existence. Scholars were literally worshipped on Spoltam, a planet that professed to value knowledge above all.

When one was decreed a scholar by the Aghni tribunal, doors opened. People listened. Invitations never stopped coming to one's door.

Yes, he had a very comfortable life.

The corners of his sensual mouth curved up ever so slightly. *An interesting life, indeed.*

He bent over the stone railing and idly watched a pretty young maiden make her way to the marketplace, basket in hand.

He was not as interested as he should have been.

Lately, there had been *something* niggling at him.

What it was– he could not say.

He only knew that it kept him up through the hours of night and nagged at him through the hours of day. Scholars were often plagued by obscure conundrums that needed to be solved; yet, Daxan knew that was not the reason for his odd affliction.

This irritation was almost *cajoling* him.

Thus far, he had been able to contain the feeling so it had not interfered with his work. But if that changed, he would be forced to take drastic action.

Strange, but the prospect saddened him.

Still, he knew what he had to do.

His golden eyes scanned the horizon. Even now he could feel its strange lure.

Calling. . . Always calling. . . .

She had done it!

Soosha looked around in disbelief. The strange alien city was gleaming in the bright sunlight!

Just waiting for a Familiar to explore!

The plan had gone almost too smoothly, she had made the jump from M'yan to the Aviaran Hall of Tunnels with ridiculous ease. Attaching herself to a group of Aviaran delegates and their families, she had slipped effortlessly through the portal.

It had not been as simple on Aviara; but nothing she could not handle.

At first she had been overwhelmed by the Hall of Tunnels. The great gaping maws stretched on and on, in what seemed like an endless fractal of choices.

At one point, someone did try to question her and a Charl knight had called out. Alarmed, she had dashed directly into the first Tunnel on her right. The knight who had called out ordered her to stop, but she charged on and through the portal before he could stop her!

There was no clue as to what she would find on the other side, so Soosha thought it was all rather brave of her.

Now she stared wide-eyed at the stone city before her. The white buildings were so bright they almost hurt her eyes.

People bustled back and forth– some on the backs of strange animals. Soosha felt sorry for the animals who had to bear such a heavy burden. It did not seem right to her.

At first glance, some of the people did not seem very friendly, either.

On M'yan everyone was greeted with a happy smile. Here, several people– and they did look much like her in form– sneered as they passed by. As though they thought themselves somehow better than her.

An agitated group of men walked by carrying scrolls. By the way they flailed them about, they seemed to be discussing whatever was written in the tightly rolled documents. They paid little attention to where they were going; they noticed only each other and the documents they were waving in their hands. Soosha thought they would surely tumble over one another at any moment.

Which could prove very entertaining.

Her eyes gleamed in anticipation.

But the men somehow made it through the causeway, turning the corner in a flurry of jabbing elbows.

Disappointed, Soosha turned away.

Across the roadway, a woman and two children were bringing food to a man who had been tied up and forced to stand in the sun.

Soosha had never seen anything like that before.

"He will learn his lesson now!" An old woman muttered behind her. Soosha's Aviaran translator device worked perfectly; she understood every word the woman spoke.

"How can he learn his lesson if he is tied up to roast in the sun?" Soosha asked her, earnestly.

The woman clicked her tongue and gave her a sour face for an answer. "Impertinent commoner!" she sneered, then moved on.

What had the man done to be treated so? Soosha's brow furrowed. The sight deeply upset her.

She scanned the city square.

A large fountain bubbled in the center. Off to the right several men in similar dress milled about, looking for something to do. They were not knights but they had the look of fighting men.

In another area, a man was kicking his mount repeatedly until the beast let out a wail of pain. The dejected animal could not defend itself against the viscous onslaught.

This is terrible! Without thinking Soosha ran over to help the poor beast.

"You there, girl, get away! What do you think you are doing?"

"You are hurting her! Why do you whip her so?" she cried out.

"Are you mad? Get back to your master!" The man brought the tip of his lash smartly down on her shoulder.

Soosha gasped. More in shock than in pain.

"I said get back!" The lash stung her again.

Outrage overcame all else; she flung back her hood and hissed angrily.

The man instantly reared back in fright. "What the–?"

Then his eyes widened in conjecture. His expression

immediately turned to one of greed.

Ah, Soosha, look what you have done now. This does not look so good for you. She waited to see what the man would do, hoping he wouldn't–

He called out to the group of men dressed in uniforms who were standing around the central fountain. "Guards! Seize her! She has stolen my ring!"

The guards smiles died on their faces as one by one they turned to stare at her. Time froze as it sunk into their collective minds what the man had said. Now they had something *to do.*

As one, the previously bored guards began running towards her. Several seemed to be brandishing some kind of weapon!

Soosha blinked for a fraction of a second before coming to an important conclusion: *Run!*

Realizing she might have made in a mistake in choosing this particular world to explore, she sprinted through the square, then dashed into a marketplace where several stalls had been set up for traders.

Not stopping to think, she careened past a rapid blur of clothing items, a table displaying glinting weapons, baskets of fresh baked goods (they smelled enticing but she had no idea what they were and was not about to stop to find out); she was in full run. . . until she sideswiped a stall piled high with boxes of strange, speckled fruits.

The jarring action caused the stall tenting to warble.

A pole, which hadn't been securely tied, came loose; it crashed into a tray sending the tray and its contents skyward.

Large, round fruits were rolling everywhere!

Two of them bounced onto the baked goods table,

flattening half of the merchant's items in one stampeding pass.

He let out a wail of outrage.

At his scream, a beast similar to the one she had been trying to help, stomped a fat, round paw down (despite everyone screaming for him not to) right on to one of the runaway fruits.

A tremendous stench filled the air.

A huge groan from the bystanders overtook the clacking noise of the rushing guards and the din of the marketplace gone wild.

Everyone began running then– simply to get away from that horrific smell!

Why would they even sell something like THAT? Soosha wondered as she continued to dash in and around stalls, dodging her pursuers.

She was starting to enjoy herself in the chase. Soosha, like others of her kind, loved to be chased. Even more than that, she loved not getting caught!

Unless she *decided* it might be fun to be caught.

Although. . . it might not be good to be chased in this way. Her pursuers might not have her sense of humor.

"*Stop, thief!*" Her false accuser was still in hot pursuit. His jowls slapped against his red neck as he chugged after her. She swore the flabby pouches grew with each footfall.

Soosha had no doubt that when she hissed at him, he began to wonder if she could possibly be a female from the highly sought after and endlessly talked about feline race of shapeshifters.

Just the *idea* had sent him after her.

She had not raised her eyes to him, so he could not know for certain. If she could elude him, he might convince himself that his speculation was merely a maddened thought on an overly warm midday.

She dashed forward at full speed.

Daxan had entered the marketplace in a distracted mood.

That *unsettled* feeling had come back.

It seemed to intensify as he entered the stalls. And it irritated him.

He could not chance any distractions! His current work was too crucial to be waylaid by some obscure *thing* that was plaguing him. As a scholar–

He frowned as a commotion roared up near the center fountain.

Seven guards were giving chase to a female cloaked in a green cape!

Amazed, he watched the woman rapidly dash between the stalls then leap on top of a tarp. Fleet of foot and fancy free.

Over the din of commotion, he heard her. . . *delighted laughter?*

As if she were actually enjoying causing the calamity.

His golden eyes narrowed.

By the blood of Aiyah, do not let this be happening...!

Even as he uttered his heartfelt entreaty, he was forced to recognize that, indeed, it was happening.

And now it had fallen upon him to control it.

Pivoting around, he disappeared like a mist into the maze of alleyways which bordered the marketplace.

Soundless. Deadly.

***

Two of the guards that had split off to come at her from opposing directions, rushed Soosha from either side.

She grinned.

Surely, they have got to be jesting; such a tactic would fetch nothing but air!

Laughing as she agilely leapt over several boxes, she ran fleetly across the top of a tarp over a merchant's stall. *This foolish pursuit could actually become enjoyable!*

Swinging down, she plopped onto a cage of some cawing, winged beasts. They seemed to be cheering her on.

With one swipe, she kicked out at the latch, releasing the squawking, fussing prisoners, who took up the challenge like miniature feathered Charl. They boldly jumped directly into the path of everything coming headlong towards them and her.

It was a beautiful sight to behold!

And she would have gotten away too–

If a strong hand hadn't suddenly shot out of nowhere and clasped her wrist to yank her smartly into an alleyway.

Before she had a chance to recoup, a voice as silky as the fabric of her jatal-riaz murmured low in her ear. "Do you have any idea what the penalty is for stealing from a highborn?"

Soosha tried to catch her breath as she looked up into the face of her decisive captor.

She confronted masculine features of perfect angles and hardened edges. Golden, serious eyes framed by thick, ebony lashes; and firm lips tilted with sensual secrets that begged to be bitten into release.

At such a tempting masculine display, Soosha's own lips parted in unconscious response.

The man's hair fell far below his shoulders; the strands

were twisted from scalp to ends into long, handsome locks that were woven-bound throughout by black leather laces. Beaded coils hung at the ends.

His hair color matched his eyes. . .and yet, its true tone was difficult to tell in the weave of his hair. She suspected the strong sun of lightening some of the strands; for the golden color shaded from dark to light.

He was beautiful.

And since she came from a race that produced males of staggering beauty, that was saying much.

Perhaps she should tell her female friends of this place?

Still, he had no right to stop her. "How do you know I do not know the laws here?"

His golden eyes–quite beautiful, really, even though they were both the same color– hardened into sharp flints of disapproval.

Soosha rather liked that, too. Such a stern expression could only be an invitation to play!

"If you did know our laws, you would not have stolen from that Cezarim."

"I have not stolen from him. He speaks falsely!"

"And who do you think the guards will believe? A wealthy townsman from a seasoned family or you, an off lander?"

Soosha looked to the right to avoid answering the question directly. On M'yan, the feline tactic was called *shinar y shinjii*, which roughly boiled down to: 'I do not hear you because I choose not to'.

The stubborn ploy had no effect on him whatsoever. Her captor's austere expression did not waver.

His grip on her arm remained firm.

"Allow me to enlighten you, visitor. Spoltam does not

abide criminals. We have little crime here because most offenses are viewed equally in this land and, thus, are punished in the same fashion." He paused to let his next word have its effect. "Death."

"*Death*?" Soosha gasped, suitably impressed. "But I have only just arrived!"

Daxan tried not to smile at the charming response. It was not easy under the circumstances. "So, should we give you more time, then, to cause real trouble and be executed?"

Her mouth dropped open. "I. . ."

"Why have you come here?"

"Wh-what do you mean?" She gazed straight at his chest. Well, it was partially bared and right in front of her. She could not help it. Broad and muscular, smooth golden skin like the finest. . .

Daxan frowned. The woman was not focusing on his warning. He lifted her chin with his forefinger. Pushing back the hood of her cloak, he stared at her face.

Delightfully distracted by his overwhelming masculinity, Soosha gazed up at him in return.

Daxan lips parted slightly as he examined her features. The woman was exquisite! Her beauty held the promise of steaming nights and playful, teasing days.

Yet it was her eyes that promised *much* more. One blue and one gold, slightly tilted, they held liquid, exotic promise.

They were arresting.

Daxan tried to exhale slowly. This was a Familiar woman! *How had she come to be on Spoltam?*

He glanced over his shoulder to make sure no one had seen her.

Quickly, he lifted the hood back up over her face. "It

would be best if you are not seen. There have been some Oberion slavers in the marketplace of late."

So he had already discovered her secret. At times, Familiars, like all felines, could be distracted by the oddest things. But then their males had the uncanny ability to *focus* on something or someone to the exclusion of all else. Taj Gian never became distracted and her brother– What did this man just say?

Soosha sucked in her breath as his words replayed in her mind. *Slavers*? Her nostrils flared in anger. "Why do you allow it?" She personally accused him.

"I do not allow it. Or disallow it. It has nothing to do with me."

She snorted in disgust. "A typical response! When they come for you, then it will have to do with you, hmm?"

Daxan said nothing; he just watched her intently.

The man had the disarming stare of a very knowledgeable man. Soosha did not like that one bit. She tugged at her arm to free it.

He held fast.

She was close to a snarl. "What is this horrible planet? I need to know its name so I will be sure to not come here again!"

This time the edges of his lips did curl up. "It is called Spoltam and if you think this a harsh place, you have not traveled much. Spoltam prides itself on being the most civilized of worlds."

"*Civilized*? You condone executing someone simply because a wealthy man from one of your older families claims she has stolen a trinket. You call that civilized?"

"I did not say I condone it. I am merely explaining our way of life to you lest you find yourself in a position to be executed on a daily basis."

She rubbed her chin. "I am not sure there is humor in that."

A line of amusement carved into his cheek. "One would not think so. Spoltam's elder families do have control– especially over this city. You would do well to remember that as well. Aghni is our main city of scholarly pursuit. While it is true our citizenry is categorized– and you may think some of us have undue privilege over others– you must understand that it is the scholars who keep the Blessed Knowledge of Spoltam alive. Scholars devote all their time to study so they can spread the word of Sense to all."

"Yes, I have already seen the sense of your scholars. There is a man tied up in the square, left to stand broiling in the sun! I was told it was so he could learn his 'lesson'."

"He is a servant who disobeyed his master."

"Oh, well then, never mind." She slammed the toe of her boot into the dirt. "Of course he does not matter. What am I thinking? Oh, and where is the nearest portal off of this disgusting world?"

A flash of white teeth in the briefest of smiles let her know he was truly amused by her. "What is your name?" he drawled as he released her arm.

Soosha lifted her chin. "I do not I think I shall tell you."

Daxan crossed his arms over his chest. "Oh, I think you shall."

"I think not. Just point me towards the nearest Tunnel and I shall leave this wretched place forthwith."

"You are not returning to M'yan?"

Soosha faltered. He knew of her homeworld? She was not sure, but she did not think many outsiders knew much of her homeworld. Or that it was called M'yan.

The least that was said about her world and her people, the better.

"No, I am a traveler." That felt good to say, even if her journey had only just begun.

"Did not your King order all Familiar home?"

"How do you know that?" The admission slipped out and it was too late to call it back.

"I am known to several High Guild members on Aviara. The Alliance hopes to entice Spoltam into their fold, so I am kept apprised of everything that might affect us."

"Who are you?"

"I am called Daxan Sahain and you have not answered my question."

She shrugged.

He arched an eyebrow at her. "Let me guess. You want to adventure, so you defied the royal decree?"

Soosha responded with the *shinar y shinjii*.

"You are not planning on going to M'yan, are you?" It was more statement than question.

"No. I told you, I am a traveler."

"*Mmm.* Yes, you have journeyed all the way from M'yan to Spoltam– where you have been for, perhaps, a few moments."

"How did you know that?" She swore under her breath as she realized he had tricked her again into giving him more information! Soosha wondered where he was headed with this interrogation!

She did not have to wait long to find out.

"I am taking you home."

That said, the tall man clasped her wrist and started striding through the maze of alleyways. Hauling her along behind him.

"*Wait*! What are you doing?" Soosha tried to dig in her heels and pull her hand free at the same time.

Against the strength of such a man it was useless. Her boot heels left deep furrows in the dirt as she was dragged along.

"I cannot take you back to your people now; nor can I, in good conscience, let you venture into sure danger. You will remain in my home until I am able to return you to your family– no doubt they are ill with worry over you."

He continued tugging her along.

"You have no right to do this!"

"I am trying to help you. Believe me, the Tunnel to the next world is one *you* particularly would not welcome; although they would welcome you with ropes and chains. Ganakari links directly to Spoltam, you foolish girl, and if you know not what place that is, then you are truly naive."

"I have not heard of this Ganakari!"

"So I thought. Your family protects you against the horrors Familiars face offworld. Ganakari is where your king was recently imprisoned. *And* it is where they amass an army to hunt down those like you."

He picked up his pace.

Soosha had no intention of going with this stranger! For all she knew, *he* could be a slaver.

Furthermore, he was wrong.

She knew of the plight of her people.

Soosha sighed. She also knew that her elder brother, Brygar, had a tendency to shield her. Familiar males were ridiculously protective over their family members. While she had known that taj Gian had been captured and had executed a daring escape, she had never been told the name of the planet he had been held captive on.

41

But that had naught to do with this stranger. "Stop this! I am not a child seeking your protection! Let me go!"

"Be quiet! You are putting us both at risk! I do not wish to have to plea for you if that Cezarim finds us."

Soosha disagreed. She began to fight in earnest.

Not one to quibble, Daxan stooped down, placed a broad shoulder against her midsection and tossed her over his back.

Familiar females did not take well to being handled without their consent.

Soosha proceeded to claw and scratch his back. In such a state, the females of her kind were tempests of fury. Most wold have dropped her and ran for their lives at the outset of the fit.

This man did not so much as miss a step.

Is he made of stone? Soosha was furious. "I am not your concern! Let me go!"

"Oh, you are my concern, all right, and I have no intention of letting you go." With those cryptic words, he smartly slapped her behind with the flat of his hand.

Whap!

Soosha could not believe he would have the audacity to do such a thing! After all, she was almost a member of the royal family. How dare he!

Daxan ignored her yells of outrage and kept walking.

Three things occurred to Soosha simultaneously as she bit a chunk of the man's back.

The first two made her spitting mad. The third gave her pause.

First, she believed herself extremely ill-fortuned to have come upon someone straightaway on this world who felt duty-bound to 'safeguard' her.

Second, she did not think she was going to talk, cajole, or otherwise sweeten this man into releasing her until he heard otherwise from her family; or from *taj* Gian himself. She had seen *that* in his golden eyes. All of a sudden, she wondered just how angry *taj* Gian was going to be over this escapade? She had disobeyed a directive from her king. . .

And finally– and this was without a doubt the worst of the three revelations– this non-Familiar, unreasonable stranger. . . seemed to be. . .

Her mate.

By the blood of Aiyah! Familiars always had the innate ability to sense these things; unfortunately, she had discovered the disturbing fact a fraction of a moment *after* she had sunk her teeth into the muscular curvature of his back.

The bite had not been a love nip.

Not even close to a love nip.

Soosha did not think her actions would particularly endear her to this Spoltam stranger, who would know nothing of Familiar ways.

She shrugged fatalistically. One must do what one must do. She bit him again. Harder.

At the sharp sting of her teeth, Daxan sucked in his breath then let it out in a *whoosh*.

Soosha waited to see what he would do. She knew what a Familiar man would do– either growl or bite her back. Maybe both.

And not necessarily with displeasure.

Daxan Sahain did neither.

His step barely faltered as he marched along with her bobbing on his shoulder. "If you do that one more time," he cautioned in a low voice, " you will regret it."

43

She tended to believe him. As a warning, his tone was fairly potent. And there was something about him that told her that he never cautioned idly.

Soosha's brow knit in puzzlement.

She only knew the ways of Familiar men– who could be very formidable when irked. She knew absolutely nothing about Spoltam males.

Do they growl when they are angry or aroused? Do they purr when they are feeling very sensual or content?

And why ever was she a match to *him*?

Familiars rarely mated outside their species. She was not sure how she felt about this sudden change in her life.

The man was certainly comely, yes, but she was not seasoned enough to mate. Surely she needed more time to play about? Of course she did!

Moreover, why was she sensing him when it was usually the male that first triggered the response in the female?

The only Familiar woman she knew of that had mated outside of their people was Rejar's mother, Suleila. What could she recall about that mating. . .?

Suleila had said that it was Krue who relentlessly pursued her. Soosha was not sure, but it had sounded as if Suleila had no idea Krue was to be her mate, at least not at first.

Familiar mating ritual was very complex; Soosha did not pretend to understand its intricacies.

She shrugged fatalistically in the philosophical way of her kind. The Familiar gesture said, 'it is upon me now, so I will deal with it now'.

She froze mid-shrug.

Oh no! He will not be able to gift me with the 900 strokes to love!

Soosha eyes widened at such a distressing thought. From what she had heard, *that* was a lot for a woman to give up!

On the other hand. . . mayhap Spoltam men had their own delights to share?

The idea immediately perked her up.

What if this Spoltam male does not wish to mate with me? Soosha worried her lip. He was not Familiar; he would not know he was to be her lifelong companion.

Should she tell him?

At the moment, it did not seem as if he would embrace the news. Especially since she had just bitten a chunk of his back.

Mayhap she should wait a while before informing him they were to spend the rest of their lives together?

And that he must be true to her forever. Just like a Familiar man.

Yes, she would give him a little time to learn of her; then he would have to mate her.

Feline in temperament, it never donned on Soosha that the man would not cherish her. A Familiar's attitude could often be summed up as: "I have decided to be in your presence; of course you must adore me!"

Having thought through her present dilemma, Soosha relaxed against the man's broad shoulders. "You can let me down now; I have decided to go with you to your home." She made her voice sound especially sweet.

Daxan arched his eyebrow. "Just like that, hmm? Had a change of heart, have you?" He did not let up his hold on her for an instant.

"Yes, actually I have. Your words have sense and if I am a guest in your home, I will have a better chance of learning of your people. It is the reason I am traveling, after all.

Now that I have calmed down, I see the benefit in what you suggest. Since you are well known to the High Guild– and my senses tell me you speak the truth– I no longer have qualms about going with you. You may release me."

There. It was a good proclamation. And reasonable, too. Soosha could have purred at her own fine sense; humility not being an attribute of her kind.

"I think not, my lady Familiar."

She could not believe her dainty little ears. "Wh-what did you say?"

"I believe you heard me correctly– but allow me to explain: I do not like being ordered about. I have even less liking for being told what I will and will not do. You have made your declaration; I am having trouble trusting in your words."

The line of her back arched up as her integrity as impugned. "That is ridiculous! Familiars do not lie!"

"Keep your voice down!" he hissed. "Do you wish others to know of you as well? Have you no sense of the danger?"

Her arm sliced the air, dismissing his concerns. "Adventuring is always fraught with danger. That is what makes it so delightful."

"Mmmm. You are either very naive or very foolish." He rested his chin against the back of her upper thigh. The skin was remarkably smooth; it was all he could do not to nuzzle against it. "I am wagering it is both."

Her nostrils flared at the insult. This Spoltami man was quite vexing!

Sometimes that can be a good thing, Soosha. . .

She thought about it. Familiar woman generally loved complexity in their males. She just was not sure she liked the trait in *him*. After all, he was not Familiar!

He had no right to be so vexing.

It might be better all around if he was not so difficult. Generally speaking, she could charm a bowl of calan stew from a starving man. This man, however, might be somewhat more difficult to manage. . . .

As if to prove her assessment, Daxan choose that moment to suddenly bite *her* on the thigh.

Soosha's mouth dropped open at the sharp, sensual sting of his teeth.

The hot nip sent shivers up her leg.

Other women might be offended by what this man had done; she admired him for it. His reaction hinted that he might be a passionate lover and that pleased her.

Still, she needed to set her boundaries. Her kinswoman, Suleila, had once instructed her on these important matters of life. 'Begin as you mean to go on,' Suleila had told her.

Of course, later Soosha had found out that it had actually been Suleila's mate, Krue, who had impressed such wisdom on Suleila.

No matter. Good advice was good advice.

"You go too far Daxan Sahain." Even to her own ears her protest was rather tepid.

Daxan smiled slowly. "No, my lovely Familiar woman, *I reciprocate.*"

With that warning, he skirted past a side gate of a stone-walled dwelling. Soosha barely had a glimpse of a small garden before they went through an arched stone doorway. The plantings were quite colorful in this area; she would have enjoyed investigating their interesting scents but he did not stop.

Inside, the floor was a tumbled mixture of polished stones.

47

Through an open doorway, Soosha got a brief glance of someone cooking as they passed. A rather rounded *Zot*. Soosha had heard that *Zots* were native to the planet Zarrain. They were highly sought after as cooks, but they were extremely sensitive about the responsibilities of properly feeding those they served.

This one was swinging both snout and tail in syncopated rhythm as he clattered several pots about in blissful preparation of a meal.

Daxan whisked her past several additional open chambers and then up a wide stairway. Jouncing her all the way.

The dwelling seemed rather large to her. "Is this entire dwelling your home?" Familiars were known for being overly, sometimes inappropriately, inquisitive.

She could feel Daxan smile against her thigh. "Yes."

"What will your family think of you bringing me home like this?" Soosha already knew he was not mated, she was referring to his blood relatives.

"My family does not reside here."

His response perplexed her. Familiar families loved to live together– every day brought plenty of opportunity for squabbles! What would life be without the friction of your family to irk you along? Who better to annoy than your closest loved ones?

"You do not live with your family?" Her tone was so endearingly concerned that his hand involuntarily caressed the curve of her backside.

"Spoltam adults live in their own domiciles. Families grow out and apart."

Soosha was horrified. "But-but how could you live without those you love around you? Who is there to share

48

your happiness and woes? Where do you find someone to fight with that you know will have to forgive you? *Who do you irritate*?!"

Her shocked, innocent inquiries were exceedingly humorous to him.

He chuckled. "We can always find someone to bother, I assure you. As for our lives, Spoltami believe in the sanctity of the individual. True originality and development can only be achieved when all familial influences are removed."

Soosha was thunderstruck. "That is not right! Familiars are very independent–"

"So I have heard."

"Yet we put great faith in our families."

Daxan shrugged. "It is a different viewpoint."

"Do you not see your parents? Your brothers and sisters?" She could not imagine such a thing.

He seemed to reflect on that for a moment. "Of course we do. We have festivals and visits. But our day to day lives are kept separate."

"And you enjoy this?"

He paused. "It is the way it is."

She was to learn that was a typical Spoltam reply.

Nonetheless, Soosha let him know exactly how it was going to be with them. "Well, my family will always be a part of my life!"

He gave her an odd look. Then tried to explain further. "Our perspective is different from yours. Spoltami put much store in knowledge. A man must study his entire life. Some of us achieve what is called "exalted thinking." We become sanctioned scholars. That is our highest aim."

Such a dispassionate objective was totally alien to her

way of thinking. "What good is this knowledge without a foundation of loving support?"

Daxan opened his mouth to reply but nothing came out.

Her simple question was not so simple. He was impressed with her natural acuity. "I will have to think of a reply to that one."

"You do that." She grinned in a gamin way. Teasing. Alluring. *Catlike.*

They continued down a long hallway and through a wide arch which led directly into a massive sleeping chamber.

Daxan deposited her there, flinging her upright with a *whoosh!*

"I have something I must attend to. I will be back after the sun sets. In the meantime, the servants will bring you whatever you wish."

"Very well."

"Since you trust me well enough to come willingly to my home, perhaps you can tell me your name?"

She bit her lip as she weighed his request.

Not because she was not going to tell him.

Sometimes, for no discernible reason at all, Familiars hesitated. They were always instinctually, careful.

"Soosha." She finally relented. "It is Soosha."

"Hmmm. . ." He seemed to consider her name. "It suits you."

"How so?"

"I must go." He left before she had a chance to ask any more questions, closing thick wooden doors behind him.

A *click* indicated he had locked them.

So he bid her trust him, yet did not trust her! Soosha was actually more irritated with the locked doors than with the issue of trust. Familiars hated to be confined.

She tried to will herself not to pace.

Mayhap she could distract herself by threshing out the room? A healthy dose of curiosity never killed the cat, for information always wooed her back!

Soosha chuckled as she set out to explore the area.

Planet Aviara, House of Sages, High Guild

"I believe that concludes our affairs for today."

The wizard Gelfan, current leader of the High Guild, attempted to put an end to another long, torturous meeting in the House of Sages.

The meeting had been a typical one in that not much was actually accomplished.

The Guild seemed to be achieving less and less as time went by.

Perhaps, Yaniff thought, *I am being unfair? Matters just seem to take longer these days.*

The House of Sages, always rife with endless discussions, ponderings, musings, and bickering, seemed especially ineffective of late. Yaniff wondered why it had come to this. In any case, they were not done for today.

Not nearly done.

"Not yet, Gelfan." Yaniff leaned forward in his chair.

Some of the wizards had already begun to rise from their seats. With Yaniff's words, a general creaking ensued as old bones wearily retook their chairs. Whenever Yaniff spoke, it was known throughout the High Guild that more was coming.

He was a seventh-level mystic– there was no telling *how much more* was coming.

Grumbled murmurings filled the hall.

The sounds of old, responsible wizards in weighty debate were identifiable and predictable.

They were a resigned lot.

Bojo, Yaniff's winged-companion, chortled gleefully.

Yaniff, tried not to smile as he stroked Bojo's feathers in acknowledgment. Yes, they were a predictable bunch of old 'coots', as Adeeann would often say.

Gelfan, a shrewd, perceptive manipulator, raised his brow as if he had mistakenly overlooked this last bit of a problem.

Yaniff knew better.

These days, he watched Gelfan most carefully.

"Ah, yes. The matter of that Familiar girl. . . What was her name again?"

Gelfan had not forgotten her name. Nor the situation. "Soosha." Yaniff replied succinctly.

"Ah, yes, Soosha. I understand she has taken it upon herself to 'run off' M'yan. I hardly see where this is a matter of concern to the High Guild, Yaniff. If this young woman decided to go against her king and put herself in jeopardy, it is really none of our concern."

Yaniff raised his eyebrow. "Then perhaps it is *you* who will tell that to her brother who now awaits our decision outside this very chamber?"

Several of the wizards snickered.

They *all* were quite aware that the robust Familiar was beyond the closed doors of the High Guild chamber. They had been subjected to his constant pacing and grumbling since their meeting began at midday. It was early eve and the man was still out there stomping and, every now and then, vocally letting them all know of his presence.

His select choice of words were attention-getting, to say the least.

Gelfan frowned, waving his hand in dismissal. "Yes, we all know the man is outside the chamber."

Yaniff felt a duty to the distressed Familiar. "Since he learned of his sister's whereabouts on Spoltam, all manner of thoughts go through his head. You should not make light of his concern, Gelfan."

Gelfan showed no remorse at his harsh judgement. "I understand that this brother, *Brygar*, is quite a brash, impatient man. Some say he has the temperament of a *xathu*."

Several of the wizards chuckled at the apt description. Even now they could hear the man bellowing out in the hall.

Gelfan could be most charming when he wanted to be. *Such charm is always dangerous.* Yaniff acknowledged that the wizard could become a serious concern. . .

He pulled himself up out of his chair, leaning heavily on his staff. Some statements required a little higher vantage point.

Especially in this chamber.

"It is true that Brygar can roar on occasion; at times, he is a most daring, impulsive Familiar– but his heart is true.

He worries over his sister. Knowing what captured Familiars endure, does anyone blame him?"

Yaniff's chastising words instantly sobered up the chamber. Ernak, a kindly old mystic, nodded his head in agreement. "Their situation is most dreadful."

Gelfan sighed loudly. "Yes, of course it is dreadful, *however*, let us not confuse the issue with over-sentimentality. We all know the situation of the Familiar. This esteemed council has oft acknowledged our agreement to aid them. Yet this particular incident has been brought about by one girl who took it upon herself to disobey a direct order of their king, Gian Ren. What is more, the brother, Brygar, is insisting that he accompany any Charl warrior we might choose to send. If we decide to send a Charl. And I might add, he is *demanding* that we do so."

Gelfan paused to let his piercing stare capture each member. The knifelike expression clearly conveyed that the Familiar's behavior toward such a revered body as the House of Sages was sheer audacity.

Yaniff watched the scene unfold before him, silent as a stone.

Gelfan continued his speech. "I say we let it be. With his rash behavior, this Familiar is likely to cause a planetary incident that we can ill afford. The ruling council on Spoltam, the Reign, will take immediate offense to what they will perceive as his instinctual, emotional feline temperament."

Wolthanth, one of the wisest wizards in the High Guild, disagreed. "You are wrong, Gelfan. Brygar will undoubtedly go after his sister with or without our aid. Best it be with our aid– if only to have some control over him."

Yaniff nodded to Wolthanth to thank him for his support. Gelfan was not known for his strong advocacy of the Familiar. The feline race had no champion in him. Yaniff well remembered that Gelfan had not been happy to discover that Rejar, the half-Familiar son of Krue, had in fact, inherited prophetic Charl powers.

Rejar's first act as a newly indoctrinated Charl had been to align Gelfan's house to him by accepting his Cearix. It had been a shrewd maneuver and Yaniff had later commended his student for it. In time, Rejar would learn to read that dagger's 'truth'.

Yaniff sighed. It was unfortunate that when the Familiar needed the guiding hand of the Sages the most, a man such as Gelfan led the High Guild. His powers of persuasion were strong. He could turn many of the Sages; and they would cast their votes with him.

Zysyz, the newest member of the House of Sages interrupted the path of Yaniff's thoughts with his first *interesting* comment.

"Excuse me, but, how does Spoltam stand on the issue of Ganakari?"

Yaniff raised his eyebrows. Mayhap he had passed over Zysyz too soon? Mayhap there was yet a future ally here...

With the proper underpinning, of course.

Gelfan, somewhat surprised at Zysyz astute question, answered. "Spoltam shares a Tunnel annex point with Ganakari. The Spoltami, with their highly developed systems of lucid reasoning, naturally feel that the Familiar, a race that relies heavily on instinct and emotion, are somewhat inferior."

Yaniff noted Gelfan's use of the word 'naturally'. Bojo brushed the edge of his beak lightly against Yaniff's earlobe.

"They are biased, but not overtly hostile to the race as a whole. So far, they have not joined into a pact with Ganakari. Although, that could change at any time. Which makes this situation all the more delicate."

Yaniff corrected Gelfan's glossed over summary. "They do allow slavers access to their planet."

Several of the wizards frowned disapprovingly.

Wolthanth stroked his chin. "I have always wondered how the Spoltami manage to allow their 'lucid' reasoning to condone such a thing; yet, it seems they are equally enamored of *privilege*."

"They are not part of the Alliance," Gelfan shot back. Slavers were strictly forbidden in the Alliance. "If we ever hope to bring them into the Alliance then we need tread carefully."

"This is a crucial balance." Ernak added the obvious– but in a wise-sounding voice.

Yaniff groaned inwardly. Ernak was an extremely kind wizard who did not have the heart for decisive action.

"Spoltam favors us." Gelfan pressed his point. "Let it be known that their scholars spend much time interpreting adages from the House of Sages."

Wolthanth winked at the table. "Yes, I have heard that a Spoltami scholar can cheerfully spend years interpreting a single sentence of Charl *mystic-chatter*. Knights, our quest for obscurity is well met!"

Despite the seriousness of the situation, they all laughed. Even Bojo cawed.

Immediately, a deep voice bellowed outside and the complaint reached them clearly in the council chamber– right through wooden doors that were almost as dense as the tree trunks in the Towering Forests. *"Laughing?! They laugh while my sister languishes on a pretentious planet of kiss-slavers!"*

Many of the wizards raised their brows.

Yaniff winced. *He helps not his cause.*

He knew his assessment was correct when Brygar's tirade against 'overly prudent, dawdling wizards' rose to new heights. *"I dare not ask myself how long it takes them to relieve themselves, for surely they must discuss the function for hours before finding the proper direction to do so!"*

Several of the Sages began to frown. Deeply.

Yaniff saw the time was upon him. He quickly stepped forward to divert their concerns and lead them to the cause.

"Wolthanth is right; let us have some control over the incident. By carefully choosing an emissary from the Charl, we will remain in command. The key is to send someone to Spoltam who will not only find Soosha, but who will also be more than capable of *tempering* Brygar. Thus we will master the situation. I call for a first vote."

It was a brilliant tactical maneuver, coming at such a time in the daily deliberations. Late in the day, nearing the evening meal.

The words 'temper', 'master' and 'control', served up all at once, was a dish any wizard could chew on. Especially if it hastened the meeting. (Thus, the process of how some mystical decisions are ultimately rendered is revealed: Old men do not favor late evening meals.)

Most of the mystics quickly spoke in assent, giving Yaniff the quorum he needed to proceed.

Gelfan had cautiously remained neutral.

"Have you someone in mind, Yaniff?" Ernak patted his

stomach as it growled.

Yaniff smiled crookedly; Ernak's mind was more involved with pondering what choices he would be having for his meal than the subject at hand.

Bojo stretched his wings, refolding them neatly. That done, the winged companion started to snore. *Loudly.*

Yaniff shook his shoulder to wake Bojo up. *Am I the only one ever concerned with the fate of the universe?*

Bojo opened one eye.

It drifted shut again.

Yaniff snorted to himself. And boldly continued.

With all the aplomb of a seventh-level wizard who is very much concerned with the fate of the universe, he put forward an option. "As it happens, I do have someone in mind."

"Who would have guessed?" Gelfan muttered– but loudly enough for everyone to hear.

"What say you, Gelfan?" Yaniff purposely cupped his ear. "I did not quite hear you." Oh, he was being very bad. And, yes, he was enjoying it.

His rise in mood emanated to his winged-companion, who awoke and gave Gelfan a sharp-toothed grin.

It irritated Gelfan immensely.

For some reason companions generally took great delight in irking other wizards. Their expressions said: *See what you do not have? Me. Why? Because I chose a better wizard.* Companions were notoriously *wizardproud.*

Yaniff equitably concluded that there had to be some reason for enduring these sessions. If not irritating Gelfan, then what?

Gelfan was not happy with either of them; he glared at Yaniff for calling him out. So he yelled down the table. In wizard-boom.

"I BOW TO YOUR GREAT AGE AND SHALL BE SURE TO SPEAK UP FOR YOU, YANIFF. WHO IS THIS SUPREMELY HALLOWED CHARL; ONE WHO CAN KEEP SUCH A FAMILIAR IN LINE?"

Several of the mystics cupped their ears, wincing, their mugs of *mir* clattering across the wooden table with the vibration of his voice.

Yaniff was unfazed. He retook his seat. "Ah! I believe these disintegrating, worthless ears can hear footsteps approaching at this very moment."

The doors to the chamber suddenly crashed open with a deafening *bang*! Boot heels clicked an angry staccato across the stone floor.

"What mean you, Yaniff, to summon me here like some Charl supplicant to do your bidding!" Traed ta'al Krue confronted the room, glowering at the entire House of Sages.

Since the scowl was accompanied by an irritated toss of waist-length dark hair; as well as the sparking, flashing eyes of a high level mystical-warrior in his prime. . . it was rather effective.

Several Sages actually sat back in their seats.

Yaniff chuckled. *The lad cannot help the drama that follows him.* "He calls it upon himself, does he not, Bojo?"

The winged-companion squawked back in reply.

Yaniff's eyes, darker than the darkest night, glowed with mischief. "Ah, but how can I not?" He ruffled Bojo's feathers.

If Traed's unruly entrance was not enough to unsettle the venerable House of Sages, the snarling, angry, mountain of a Familiar that followed in the Aviaran's wake certainly proved sufficient.

The man continued to roar as he came into the room.

His litany of complaints were much louder now that the thick wooden doors were not between him and the Sages. Ernak and Zysyz groaned and slid down into their chairs.

Others on the chamber held the same sentiment.

"Not him!"

"Do not let that bothersome Familiar in here!"

"By Aiyah! Close the door quickly! We have been hearing his tirade all day!"

Clearly the Familiar was not a popular "guest".

The wizards' pleas were roundly ignored by the tall, dark Aviaran glowering before them. Traed's focus, however, was purely on Yaniff.

The one who had called him.

The one who always managed to embroil him in one scheme after another!

It was a mystery to Traed how this was done as he was not even a Charl supplicant.

"I see you have received my message, Traed."

If fury had a name, it would have been Traed ta'al Krue. The normally stoical Aviaran flashed warning signals with every part of his body.

Palms flat on the council table, he bent towards Yaniff. "I have oft told you," he gritted out in a deadly soft voice, "I will not be treated as a Charl supplicant. I am not here to do your bidding."

Yaniff could not have been more pleased. With his own words, Traed had just bound himself to the task at hand.

Although he did not know it.

Yet.

To a wizard, the Sages gaped at Traed, utterly aghast. Such insolence! To a high-level mystic? The lad needed some discipline!

To these Sages, Traed was an unknown commodity. They were uncomfortable with his lack of proper training; they questioned his dark heritage. Some feared his unschooled power.

If they were opposed to Yaniff before, they would side with him now. Traed's lack of respect had always been disquieting. Such an insult could never go unremarked.

Yaniff's knowing expression gave Traed pause. He had seen that expression before– right after the door to the snare shut tight.

Instantly he realized his mistake.

His green eyes narrowed ominously. "It will not work," he murmured to Yaniff.

"It already has."

"Cease all this Charl blather and tell me what is to be done about my sister!!" The huge, snarling, extremely handsome Familiar roared to the group at large. His eyes were an unusual combination– lavender and aqua. If one were to look close, one might ask how such soothing colors came to one who roared so fiercely.

Yaniff tried not to laugh. Yet, the events unfolding before him were extremely humorous.

"What does he rave about?" Traed nodded over his shoulder.

"There is a Familiar girl on the planet Spoltam. She left M'yan without permission, going against Gian's orders. This is her brother, Brygar. You will accompany him to Spoltam and see to the matter."

Traed's eyes narrowed to slits. "Oh, will I?"

"Yes, you will."

Traed cocked one eyebrow.

Yaniff grinned. "Taj Gian thanks you in advance for all of the Familiar people on M'yan, which is, if you recall, by royal decree, your *second* home. And there is the matter of the House of Lodarres– or should I say the honor of the House of Lodarres, Traed *ta'al Krue*."

Traed's nostrils flared.

But he remained silent.

"Finally, some action!" Brygar threw up his hands. "Would that I were not bleeding to death out there as I waited, for I surely would be missing three of my incarnations!"

Treads leveled a cool look of dismissal at the disruptive Familiar, but his aggressive stance had changed slightly. He exhaled a disgusted gust of air.

The entire situation was clear to him.

Yes, he was caught.

"You are a crafty old–"

With a feigned, pained expression, Yaniff shook his finger back and forth. "Ah-ah-ah."

Traed was unmoved. "You brought Gian into this knowing I am honor-bound not to refuse him!"

"Not so. Gian was already involved. He made you a member of his extended family when you saved both his life and the life of his *tajan*, Jenise. In addition, you are now a *recognized* son of Krue, a great Charl warrior."

"Occurrences which I suspect you also had much to do with, Yaniff."

"You cannot refuse this request."

Brygar was through with waiting. "Are we to leave, Charl, or stand here exchanging pleasantries all eve? Let us be off at once!"

Traed's jaw pulsed. He did not even look at the annoying

Familiar.

He did glare at Yaniff though.

And the glare said it all.

Traed would never be able to abide Brygar, let alone take a journey with him. The Aviaran was a solitary man, quiet and watchful in his way. Ever remote.

Brygar would surely drive him mad.

Yaniff chuckled, further infuriating the younger man. Traed's hand drifted over to the light saber at his waist.

Yaniff's eyes twinkled merrily. He made a wager with himself as to how long it would be before the two of them were at each other's throats. To help them along, his next words were a simple spice to steam the "throttle-stew."

"Your level head will keep him out of trouble, Traed."

And where had Traed heard that before? Ah, yes, just before Yaniff sent him off to Ree-Gen-Cee Eng-Land after Rejar. *That* escapade had resulted in him exposing his powers to the Guild!

Traed glared at Yaniff.

Gelfan, bored with the entire situation– and also hungry for his evening meal– decided to put an end to it. "Traed ta'al Krue, the Guild decrees that you will go to Spoltam and bring back this Familiar girl to M'yan.'

Traed met Yaniff's eyes. That was not exactly what Yaniff had said.

"Thus you see why I always choose you, Traed," Yaniff murmured approvingly. "You have yet to disappoint me."

"Mayhap I should work harder at it."

"Somehow, each time, I think you do," Yaniff wisely rejoined.

Traed looked at him, caught speechless and yet. . . not without words.

"Enough! I am leaving with or without you, Charl!" Brygar was already storming out of the High Guild.

"You will owe me much for this one, Yaniff," Traed gritted out.

Yaniff nodded. "Go after him now, before he causes a galaxian war."

"I do not think one Familiar can do such a thing."

"No?" Yaniff's lips twitched. "Then you know not your Familiars."

Traed exhaled noisily, then turned to follow the brash Familiar.

Yaniff grinned wickedly. "All in all, a good turn, eh, Bojo? Already they are like the best of companions."

Bojo nipped Yaniff's earlobe.

Sharply.

A wizard's laughter is a beautiful thing to behold.

If you should ever hear it–

Either laugh with him or run quickly for cover.

By the time Tread caught up with Brygar, he was already at the Hall of Tunnels.

And he was in his cat form.

There was no mistaking that great stomping animal with his shock of black hair and his lavender and aqua eyes–

The cat was even snarling to himself as he raced along!

Worse, the foolhardy Familiar was about to storm through the *wrong* Tunnel.

Traed shouted a warning. "No!"

Too late.

Without stopping, Brygar barreled forward and sprang through the portal.

Traed winced.

Of all worlds to pick– why did the fool have to pick that one? Brygar had stormed headlong onto Mollock, affectionately referred to by all as 'the mud hub'.

By Aiyah, what a dolt!

He had no choice now but to go after him.

Traed gritted his teeth and plunged through the gateway. He detested mud!

Almost as much as he detested quests.

He tumbled onto the plane of Mollock, sliding hip-deep into an endless sea of sucking mud. He took the opportunity to curse the House of Sages in twenty-two languages.

If Traed had known that the Sages had neglected to inform him that Brygar was notorious on M'yan for being a Familiar who lacked *any* sense of direction. . . he would have cursed them in forty-two languages.

Especially since the affliction never seemed to stop the stubborn feline.

Indeed, the obstinate Familiar simply ignored all those who told him he could not find his way back to his own toes on a perfectly clear day.

Who had ever heard of a Familiar with no internal sense of direction?

Certainly not Brygar.

Yaniff made his way back to his cottage in the forest.

It had been an eventful day.

Halfway home, he paused on the wooded path to peer at the upper branches of a nanyat tree.

Lying across one of the limbs, basking in the shade of the thick, dark fronds, was his student, Rejar ta'al Krue.

His *tenth* level student. Half-Aviaran and half-Familiar, he was unique in every way. No other child had ever been born of Familiar and Charl, save him. Some said his conception was miraculous. His father, Krue, however, maintained that it was just good love play.

Of course, depending on the amount of mischief his younger son caused, Krue had also claimed that Rejar was love play gone astray.

Whatever the cause of his existence, it was widely acknowledged that Rejar had a way of burrowing into people's hearts.

The scamp was well-loved by many.

A light breeze billowed the full sleeves of the pale blue shirt Rejar wore. The loose garment laced at the wrist and neck. His black *tracas* fit snugly over his lean hips and waist; the black breeches were tied and laced up the front.

The lad spends too much time undoing all of those laces; his raiment mirrors his outer nature exactly, Yaniff rued. Sleek, sinuous and utterly sensual. He was the outcome of a mixed bloodline; and yet, it was the Familiar traits that were most apparent. The cat in him was strong.

Even black leather boots seemed sleeker on him than on other men.

Ah, but he is so much more. . .

Rejar was stretched out on his side, head propped up by the palm of his hand. One long leg was casually bent at the knee. His boot heel tapped a slow staccato on the wooden branch.

He gazed languidly down at Yaniff with an inscrutable expression.

"Taking a nap, are we?" Yaniff leaned against his staff as he stared up at his student.

"It is such a beautiful day, how could I resist?" Rejar's blue and gold eyes held sparks of mischief.

"Mmmm."

Rejar chuckled at Yaniff's flat reply. "You have sent Traed on another journey."

It was not a question.

Yaniff took a moment to study his student. His Familiar blood allowed him to shield his thoughts. At times, Rejar could even withhold his thoughts from Yaniff. The ability– a powerful asset– could quickly become a liability. Yaniff was most careful with Rejar's unfolding.

"And how do you know this?"

Rejar grinned. "I happened to be in the Hall of Tunnels when I observed him chasing down a huge black cat– that looked strangely like the Familiar Brygar. I could only think of one reason *our* Traed would do such a thing. . ." He wagged his finger at the wizard. "*You* are up to your tricks, Yaniff."

Sharp as ever, he is.

"Hmph! And what were you doing in the Hall of Tunnels? I distinctly remember leaving you with a rather large tome of *Curious Tinctures* that you were to study."

Rejar coughed. "And it was very scintillating, I assure you; however, there was a most beautiful piece of Krilli cloth that I had seen at the sacri yesterday and I thought Lilac would look most beguiling in such a material, so I-"

Yaniff banged his staff. "You are mated and still you squander yourself! I do not know how it is possible!"

Rejar threw back his head and laughed. "Unlike you, old man, I have not forgotten the pleasures of the day." Rejar winked at his master. "And there can be endless pleasures in a day, Yaniff."

Yaniff just shook his head and rolled his eyes. Rejar had always been a trial to him. There was something about the lad that made him want to throttle him yet clap him on the back at the same time.

"I should send you to the Sky Lands to dwell among the barren, stormy cliffs for a season. I vow you will learn much about the joys of the day there, Rejar."

He did not respond as most students would have. He laughed. "Your threat is empty."

"Why do you say this?"

"I say this because if I were to go there– *you* would go as well. You would never let an entire season go by without reprimanding me, Yaniff. It took too long for me to agree to become your student for you to let such opportunities slip by."

Yaniff shook his finger at him. "Scamp."

"*That being so*, I do not think you wish to subject your old bones to a season in the cold, damp Sky Lands." Rejar craftily viewed the wizard from beneath spiky, black lashes. "Am I not right?"

Yaniff harumphed and crossed his arms over his chest.

Grinning, Rejar turned onto his back and lazily swatted a large nanyat frond. "Yaniff. . . tell me what makes Traed a master of the blade."

Yaniff gazed shrewdly up at his student. *Excellent, Rejar. Your indolent appearance belies your true intent.* It was a remarkable foray into subtle wizardry for one so young.

Rejar had not been fetching silken fabric for his wife; he had stepped out to investigate matters on his own. The impressive initiative earned the student the key to the next door.

His question would be answered.

"Have you ever seen Traed in a life and death battle, Rejar?"

"I have seen him fight, yes."

"That is not the same thing."

"Explain, Yaniff."

"When Traed is in a duel, he never flinches– not even when a death blow may be imminent. He never gives up. He fights with the ardor of a man who *cherishes* life. Every moment of it."

"Are you sure you speak of Traed? I have seen him put

himself directly in the path of danger without regard for his being."

"I have witnessed this as well. But I assure you, he holds all life dear. Even his own– though he recognizes it not. Still, he will willingly fight to the death. A man who embraces such conflict, whose skill is masterful, is difficult to best in any fight. He goes in with nothing *and* everything to lose. You see, Traed never fights to survive– *he fights to live*. Do you understand?"

"Yes, master. I understand."

"Good. Then know this: Traed has had powerful motivators. In battle, his terrible losses have served to strengthen his arm."

"But do they strengthen *him*? He constantly battles himself and the darkness he imagines dwells inside. In the end, this can only break him. . ." Rejar's brow furrowed. "Or. . . make him *invincible*."

Yaniff started, but would not reply. The old wizard was not often surprised. For a moment he had been caught off-guard by the younger man's incredible acuity.

Rejar thought Yaniff's reaction telling. "Perhaps I venture into a place you do not wish me to go?"

"Perhaps you would like to think that."

"Do you believe it is my destiny to master the blade, Yaniff?"

Ah, we get to the real matter at last! He worries over his destiny. Yaniff sighed. *And well he should. . .*

"You have the reflexes and skill to become a legendary bladesman. Already you have shown great promise. It remains to be seen whether your *will* carries you to those levels."

"If all you have told me is so, what losses shall then

guide *my* arm, Yaniff?"

"The hand that wields the perfect blade is guided by many things. It is how the blade is fashioned that tells the tale. You have gifts that are yet to be revealed."

"Then tell me no more. Your prophecy hangs over my head like a Cearix that has two edges of one truth; and it concerns me night and day. I already have more "gifts" than I can or want to deal with."

"From your own mouth you state the quest. You must learn to *embody* these gifts, Rejar. Willingly. They must be embraced right to your heart– or all of your training will be for naught. Do you understand what I say?"

"Yes, I understand your words and I will try to do as you say. I put all of my trust in you, Yaniff."

"Good. Then you have learned well the lesson for this day."

Rejar's lips parted; the old wizard got him again! "You *knew* I would follow you?"

Yaniff shook his head. "No. As always, I left the decision up to you, Rejar. You chose the path and, thus, your lesson."

"I see."

"Come down." Yaniff motioned him with his hand. "The day is nearing its close and the evening draws nigh."

Rejar agilely hopped off the tree limb, landing next to his teacher.

"Suleila has made calan stew for you, Rejar."

The dark-haired man grinned broadly. "I vow I have a taste for it!"

"I know– which is why I happened to mention it to her earlier today."

Rejar was surprised, yet moved by the thoughtful deed.

"You cannot hide everything from me." The wizard kindly clapped him on the back.

"Did you say everything?" Rejar scoffed. "I can hide nothing from you!"

Yaniff chuckled as they strolled through the forrest to the house of Krue. "Since you have been but a boy, I have always known when your belly whines for calan stew."

"My belly never whines– it purrs beseechingly." Two dimples kissed Rejar's cheeks.

"I vow I have a taste for the stew myself," Yaniff whispered as they walked the path. "It was all I could think of in the House of Sages today."

Rejar leveled a bland look at Yaniff. "Of that, I am not so sure."

Bojo squawked agreement as he swooped along beside them. Some winged-companions were quite fond of calan stew.

And others just liked to stir the pot.

Planet Spoltam, City of Aghni

Daxan rested his burning forehead against the cool, smooth stone of a pillar.

Her fragrance is that of the illumia night flower. . . .

His favorite scent. The heady blooms favored the moist air surrounding bodies of water and the silvery glow on moon shine.

Daxan walked outside onto one of the open-air passages that encompassed adjoining sections of the estate. The stone hallways served several purposes; they cooled down the rooms at night by allowing air to circulate freely, while the airy rooms were extensions to the indoor living areas.

This particular passage was perched against a high cliff overlooking the sea. Several chairs, tables, and sleeping couches dotted the length of it. Gauzy curtains delineated separate areas as they fluttered in the gentle wind.

Daxan trusted that the early evening breezes would cool him down. So far, they were only serving to remind him of the feathery caress of her silken tresses as they drifted down his back.

He took a deep breath.

Above him, the sky was a swirling scape of pinks and golds. Stars were beginning to light up the tinted sky; they sparkled above the port city like a carpet of magickal jewels.

Sunsets in Aghni were highly regarded. Even off-landers came to witness the spectacle.

This night, Daxan barely took note of it.

His thoughts were on the Familiar woman who was now under his protection. *Soosha.* The word meant 'a sweet presence' in one of the languages he had studied. Yes, it suited her. Her presence had filled his home; the luscious scent of illumia was clinging to him still.

Earlier, when he had first caught sight of her leaping merrily on to the stalls of the marketplace, he had been thoroughly entranced. Her lovely laugh was so playful!

But when he looked into those dual-colored eyes his heart began to pound. At once, his blood thickened and his loins responded with a strong quickening.

Oh, he had tried to control his reaction– he was a man who had much experience with women.

It mattered not where she was concerned.

His body came alive for her.

Nevertheless, he was presently dealing with a serious matter; he could not afford to become entailed. Despite her ample charms, he doubted he would have involved himself further in the situation. Except. . .

She was a Familiar woman.

Impossible to believe, yet here she was.

And she had placed herself in grave danger.

It was apparent that she had no real idea of the kind of peril that awaited her.

He did.

He knew what horrors could befall her should she be captured by the Oberions. Daxan was vehemently opposed to allowing the slave traders access to Spoltam.

Unfortunately, he was in the minority with that opinion.

That being the case, he could not leave her unprotected.

It was more than just that, though.

He was *drawn* to her.

From the instant he had gazed into those beguiling aqua and gold eyes, he had wanted to experience all manner of pleasure with her.

It was an irresistible desire.

If he took her, would she bite and claw him. . . or sweetly mewl for him to do more? Would she scream his name when he brought her to release. . . or softly call it in rising passion? Would she overflow for him while he licked up all of that beautiful fragrance. . . ?

He could do all of those things. And by the look of her, she could as well.

The question was what was he going to do about it?

Duty before pleasure.

That was the Spoltam way.

He would send her back to M'yan untouched by his hands and that would be the end of it.

A vision of satiny skin flashed across his mind. The downy touch of her floor-length hair as it glided over his shoulders and back. The lilting sound of her voice. The lush firmness of her thighs and backside.

Daxan was suddenly not sure he would be following the Spoltam way.

Rumors of Familiar beauty were not rumors. This traveler, with her sweet gamin face and sensual form, was utterly captivating. There was no sense in denying that she intrigued him.

What kind of woman left the safety of her home-world to venture forth into the unknown? Despite the fact that she was forbidden to do so by her King?

An adventuresome one.

While the males of her species traveled extensively, it was rumored that the females did not. From what he knew, very few actually left their homeworld. He had heard that most preferred to stay on M'yan.

No doubt causing trouble.

When they did travel, their males were often seen accompanying them, safeguarding them from the slavers who attempted to capture them at any cost.

Of course, conditions were much worse now.

There were rumors that Oberion slavers were even infiltrating some of the outlying Alliance planets, operating in hidden ways.

Still, he understood the Familiar desire for adventure. While the Spoltami concentrated their focus on scholarly pursuits, he had always had a taste for risk.

This predilection for experiencing the unknown manifested itself in many ways.

Some of them highly interesting to the women on this planet.

There were some special techniques in the art of loveplay that he had acquired that were considered unorthodox.

Of course, some skills one must simply be born with. . . It

was said that Familiars possessed pleasure skills so refined that with a simple touch they could have their partners shivering with longing.

Daxan wondered if this woman could actually make him, a 'well-seasoned' male, tremble with such a desire.

Despite the fact that he was a decisive, energetic lover, no one had ever claimed his control. He was too focused to relinquish that amount of power.

The High Guild of Aviara had already been informed of her whereabouts. He had seen to that. Until someone arrived. . .

Time with her could be wisely spent.

Since she was anxious to explore, mayhap, she would not mind exploring him? She had said she wished to learn of other peoples.

His white teeth flashed a rather sensual smile.

Perhaps he could interest her in what *he* had to offer? Pleasure could be a fine gift for adventurers to give each other. If his guest was willing to be adventuresome, he would make sure she would not forget him when she returned to M'yan.

In fact, he would ensure that her thoughts of him would be *fragrant* with the pleasing memories of her short time on Spoltam.

It soothed a man to know that a woman remembered him fondly.

He grinned, saluting the prospect of risk– without which many men and women would never get together.

By the blood of Aiyah, I am a philosopher as well as a scholar!

He snorted and stretched his muscles. In the setting sun.

Planet Mollock

"We come not a moment too soon, Charl! What kind of a world do they let my sister languish on?"

Brygar, in his human form, stared at the soggy plains and gray skies of Mollock with the disdainful expression of a cat that is expected to step in, well, mud.

Traed, slipping twice, finally reached the irksome Familiar, who was standing on the only dry spot on the plain. A large boulder.

With his hands on his hips, no less.

"Where is she, Charl? I see nothing here!"

Traed ground his teeth together. "That is because she is not here. Did you not hear me call out to you to halt?"

Brygar shrugged. "Of course I did. What is your point?"

Traed took a deep breath and tried to maintain his calm. He was known as a patient man. An utterly calm man.

Restrained.

Then why did his low voice sound as if it was pressed through *gharta* shells?

"If you heard me why did you not stop?"

"I saw no reason to. There has been enough tarrying already! Now, where is she?"

Traed spoke slowly so the dolt would hear his words. "She. . . is. . . not. . . here."

"WHAT? What trickery is this? Do the Sages think that—"

Traed put up his hand to stop the spectacular tirade. "The Sages have naught to do with it. *You* jumped the wrong Tunnel. This is not the right world, you fool!"

Brygar's mouth opened to deliver a scathing reply– but Traed's words finally sunk in. "Wrong world?" He looked down with a combination of curiosity and contempt.

As if the land insulted him by its presence beneath his feet.

"Is she not on Spoltam?"

Traed closed his eyes. *Give me strength.* "Yes, but this is not Spoltam. We are on Mollock."

"Hmmm." Brygar crossed his arms over his massive chest. "The information posted inside the Hall of Tunnels must be in error. You should tell them to fix it, Charl. There is no telling how many travelers they have led astray."

Traed gave him an arch look. "I can tell you exactly how many, Familiar. *None.* The information is not in error. *You* took a wrong turn in the Hall."

Brygar snorted at the ridiculous statement. "Impossible. I am a Familiar. Need I say more?"

Traed just stared at the large man.

Brygar frowned. "Since your people have led us to the

wrong place, let us go back through the Tunnel to the correct portal."

Traed pinched the bridge of his nose. "Allow me to explain further. There is *no* Tunnel point to return to at this point. We must now slog through endless expanses of mire to the next Tunnel portal, which, for your interest, is several days journey from here."

Brygar growled at that news. *Walk through mud for days?* He did not care for the opinion at all– and thus decided to ignore it. *Shinar y shinjii.* "This is not acceptable, Charl."

Traed nostrils flared as he exhaled. *Familiars!* "If you had not rushed off into the wrong Tunnel, we would not be here discussing this."

"And if you had not tarried so long arguing with all those old wizards, we would have been there already!"

At that precise moment a mudworm slithered over Traed's boot. Mollock mudworms made zorphs seem rather comely by comparison.

He had *had* enough!

His light saber cleared his belt. In the blink of an eye, the weapon was a hairsbreadth from Brygar's throat.

"Let us get one thing straight– I am not a Charl. I am here at Yaniff and taj Gian's behest. Not the House of Sages." His voice dropped to an ominous pitch. "Do not call me Charl again."

Standing stock-still, Brygar watched Traed with the heavy-lidded expression of a cat just waiting for a fight.

"Actually, there are two things we need get straight, Charl-who-is-not-Charl."

With narrowed eyes, Traed motioned with the cutting edge of the blade against the man's throat. So skilled was his hand, that he did not even nick the skin. A warning more deadly for the deftness of it.

"And what is this second matter you refer to?" The monotonous tone of Traed's voice implied that he was not the least bit interested in the response.

Brygar cocked his head to the side, boldly tempting fate and a slit throat. "If you ever point that weapon at me again, I will rip your heart out."

Traed quirked an eyebrow.

Instead of standing down, he actually seemed to be weighing the choice. "You are giving me incentive, Familiar."

Brygar's lavender and aqua eyes flashed with interest and perhaps a glimmer of amusement. "I will give you all the incentive you need *later*. First, we need find my sister. Let us be on our journey. I can always rip your heart out after she is safe at home on M'yan. Can we make this portal without supplies?"

"No. It is too far." Traed retracted the blade, returning it to his waist. "There should be some mud huts along the way that serve as trading posts for travelers."

"I hope you have something to trade, Aviaran. For I do not."

Traed started slogging a trail in the direction of the setting sun. With every step, the bog grabbed his boots, sucking them back into the mire. *Revolting.*

"Actually, I do have something to trade."

Brygar gave Traed a sideways glance as he caught up to him.

"And what, pray tell, is that?"

"*You.*"

Brygar let out a roar of laughter.

Although. . . he was not entirely sure the Aviaran was jesting.

By the odd lights in the sparking jade eyes–

Mayhap, he was not.

Planet Spoltam, City of Aghni

Daxan rapped softly on the chamber door before entering the room. If his guest was resting, he would leave without waking her.

She was standing near the open balcony. The pink sky of early evening surrounded her in a blushing halo.

He noted that she had changed into one of the gowns he had sent up earlier, along with some other items he thought she would enjoy. The crisp, rustling fabric was a melange of Spoltam colors; its design mirrored the natural beauty of the planet. Pinks, purples, deep blues, shades of gold.

The exquisite fabric suited her perfectly.

Daxan had seen highborn women wear similar gowns in Aghni, yet none looked as lovely as this Familiar woman.

Her hair hung down past her knees like an ebony cloak.

He noticed that she had woven multicolored Aghni pearl necklaces through the tresses. The criss-crossing strands of jewels formed a shimmering net over the glossy black locks.

He had heard that no other species had hair like the Familiar. He had always wondered about that. Seeing such exquisite beauty left him no doubt of it.

The *texture* set it apart.

The locks flowed over her like liquid, shimmering clouds. He knew from firsthand experience that those tresses felt even better than they looked.

He imagined the strands wrapped around his body as he made love to her. He felt the locks sliding between his thighs. Entwining his groin and buttocks as he slid languorously into her dewy heat. . .

Desire slammed through his loins.

Soosha turned away from the balcony view. "Did you want something?"

You. Daxan's lids lowered to mask his desire. "I have sent a messenger to Aviara. I am certain someone will be sent to fetch you before long."

Her lovely expression began to fade. "I wish you had not done that, Daxan Sahain."

"It needed to be done. Surely you must see this?"

"I had hopes that you would understand me."

"I do understand you. I hope that you will, in turn, understand that I have responsibilities."

She pursed her lips. No, she did not understand; but the deed was realized. There was nothing to be done for it now. "You need not lock the door, Daxan Sahain; I have told you I will stay willingly."

It was hard for him to say this, but say it he must. "How do I know I can trust you?"

The hurt look on her face almost undid him. He stepped forward to retract his words, but she spoke before he had the chance.

"If you knew anything about the Familiar, you would know that we do not lie."

"Ah. Well, I have heard your kind does speak the truth. . . and can be very creative with the *interpretation* of the words they speak."

She gave him an indignant sniff. "Where have you heard this?"

He gave her a knowing look, but would explain no further.

He is rather captivating. Soosha flushed under his steady regard. "I have given you my pledge. It should be enough."

"And so it is. Your door shall remain unlocked."

Her countenance brightened immediately. He was not such a difficult man, after all!

"Should you have a change of heart, though, remember that you have given your word. Remember also that I do have the ear of the House of Sages. I am sure you would not wish to be known throughout Aviara as a Familiar who does not keep her word."

Soosha frowned. Mayhap she was mad– he was an extremely difficult man! He just hid it well beneath his demeanor of stately manners!

Still, she wanted to sample his lips. They curved in a most beguiling way. As if they withheld delightful secrets.

And everyone knew there was nothing as beguiling to a Familiar as the possibility of secrets.

Sometimes lips spoke without speaking.

Her lips could speak silently, too. Soosha's eyes flashed

with mischief. *Trm-m-m-m*, she purred. Hands clasped behind her back, she stepped up on to the balls of her feet. The pose was considered very fetching on M'yan. It said that she wished to *play*.

Daxan blinked. Did he just read her correctly? What had caused this sudden shift in mood? She was rather. . . engaging.

"Are you. . . " He cleared his throat. "Are you hungry?"

Her grin was pure gamin. "Yes-s-s-s," she lengthened the word into something else entirely.

Daxan arched a brow. "Mmm. Good." He held out his arm to her.

She cocked her head to the side. "You wish me to gnaw on this?"

He laughed. "No, my sweet traveler ; I am going to take you on a new journey. I think you will like it."

"With such a promise, how could I refuse?" Smiling, she looped her arm around his. His skin had the warmth of sand toasting on the shore.

She had a vision of lying upon him by the sea as the cool water washed over them both. Except he would be hotter than the sand beneath them.

Much hotter.

Planet Mollock, somewhere between Tunnels

They still had not found the Tunnelpoint!

The frequent showers made yet another ap-pearance. Heavy clouds opened upon Traed ta'al Krue as he was attempting to pull his boot free from a knee-deep pit.

The tall Aviaran gazed up at the sky, expression *brewing*.

Water sluiced down on him without the slightest hint of mercy, pouring through his hair and over his skin.

In the blink of an eye he was sopping wet.

In front of him, a mudslicer jumped into the air a few feet, and dived back into the slog.

Delightful.

If he did not drown in this sea of slime, the mudslicers would soon be more than happy to bore into his drenched flesh for a satisfying meal!

Next to him, the Familiar irritant viewed the vista with a haughty expression of distaste that only he could muster. "Is the entire planet like this?"

Water dripped off of Traed's lashes. The leather thong tying his hair back gave way from the downpour. A lock of the waist-length mass streamed over his forehead to hang in front of his face.

He gave Brygar such a fulminating glare of disgust that a lesser Familiar– or one who had more sense– might have fled in terror.

Brygar simply crossed his arms over his massive chest.

"Well, Charl-who-is-no-Charl, do you not answer a simple question?"

This is why cats need nine lives. Not taking his burning eyes off the irritating Familiar, Traed wiped the mud from his mouth with the back of his hand. He attempted to toss the sodden hair out of his face.

Twice.

Each time it squished back, slapping cold and wet against his nose.

Normally, Traed was a very patient man. After one day in Brygar's company, however, he was prepared to run the Familiar through.

His eyes began to spark. Dangerously so.

When he spoke it was in a ominously soft voice. "You are determined to find that out, Familiar; I am sure."

Brygar snorted. "What is that to mean?"

Traed's jade eyes ignited like verdant kindling. "It means that if you take one more wrong turn, we might very well see if the entire planet is like this!"

Brygar growled softly. "Dare you imply that *I* have led us astray?"

Traed crossed his arms over his chest, mirroring Brygar's stance. The two faced each other like a stubborn set of bookends.

"I am not implying it. I have clearly stated it."

Brygar's nostrils flared. "I have heard that Aviarans have but one form. Is this so?

Traed gave him a measured glance.

"Pity to waste yours by insulting me."

"There is a difference between insult and fact. Best you learn it, Familiar."

"Your blade will not help you should I decide to *teach* you a lesson. Best you learn that, knight." Brygar sent a wad of mud flying into Traed's forehead.

The fool had the audacity to grin about it.

"We shall see." Traed extended his lightsaber, inviting Brygar to come and get some of it by cupping the fingers of his outstretched palm; he then motioned– not once but twice– with the tips of his curled fingers.

It gave Brygar pause.

The serious Aviaran was too confident. A brash Familiar he might be. . . but he was no fool.

He stroked his chin. "Mayhap, Charl-who-is-no Charl, you intend to use some of that Charl-that-is-not-Charl ability to best me?"

"Mayhap I do not *need* it to best you."

Brygar laughed at his arrogance. Familiars could always appreciate brazen attitudes. Even in the midst of heated battle.

Brygar rubbed the back of his neck. If he had been in cat form, the fur along the crest of his back would have been standing straight up since they had started out on the journey.

This Aviaran was rubbing him the wrong way.

No reason he should not return the favor.

Brygar wagged a finger at the knight. "Re-member, first we find my sister, *then* I rip your heart out. Agreed?"

Traed shook his head, returning his lightsaber to his belt. "Not hardly. First, you will agree to follow me and not take it upon yourself to 'find' the Tunnel for us again. Mayhap then we will have a chance to find your sister before I grow as old as Yaniff!"

"We even argue as to what we should argue about! It is impossible!" Brygar threw up his hands. "Fine. If it will get us moving again, *you* take us to the Tunnel."

"You are finally showing some sense. Follow me."

Traed took one step forward and was immediately sucked into a chest-deep mud pit.

SSSssssurrrrthwwwwuck!

Brygar arched a brow. "An odd way to find a Tunnel, to be sure. Do you wish me to follow you into that pit, Charl-who-is-no-Charl?"

The look Traed threw him was best left un-interpreted. He attempted to get out of the muck hole.

The ooze sucked him right back in.

Brygar sauntered over as if he had not a care in the world. Bending down on one knee, he made a great show of observing the situation.

Finally, he offered a bit of wisdom. "A Familiar would never fall into such a trap."

Traed threw him a murderous look.

Unfazed, Brygar continued to be helpful. "Our special senses tell us when to correct our movements before it is too late."

"Be silent! I am trying to think."

"I am simply saying that–"

Ignoring him, Traed tried once more to get out. The slime held him fast.

Brygar yawned. Purposely. "Do you, perchance, need a hand up?"

"Not from you. I will get out on my own."

Brygar shrugged and stood. "Suit yourself. I cannot tarry with you any longer; I have a sister to find." With that, the Familiar turned– *in the wrong direction, of course*– and strutted off.

Traed was flummoxed. "You would leave me here to rot, Familiar?"

Brygar stopped and spoke over his shoulder. "Do you wish my help?"

It was the wrong thing to ask this particular Aviaran. "I have told you, I can get out on my own."

Brygar– who never could claim patience as a virtue– turned and began walking swiftly towards Traed. "*Argh!* You are the most stubborn, irritating Charl I have ever–"

SSSsssssurrrrrthwwwwuck!

Traed pinched the bridge of his nose. "Did you not say Familiars would never fall into such traps?"

"Be silent! I am trying to think."

Traed gave him an ironic look. "Take your time."

Planet Spoltam, City of Aghni

The moon silvered the pink sand beneath Soosha's feet as she walked along the shoreline with Daxan Sahain at her side.

Before they left, he had stopped by the kitchens to pick up a vine basket that his *Zot* cook had packed with a meal. The snaggletoothed, long-snouted *Zot* had informed Daxan, '*I gave you much tasty food. Much exotic flavors. Much delight. But bring this Zot back his favorite basket!*'

Daxan had thanked him for his efforts and promised to return the woven container. *Zots* took their responsibilities and their possessions seriously.

Soosha had heard that if you wanted one to work for you, you had to respect their idiosyncratic ways. It was universally considered a small price to pay for such excellent service.

For the first time, Soosha took careful note of Daxan's raiment. His feet were now bare but he had donned a sleeveless white tunic that was belted snugly at his lean waist. Black leather *tracas* molded his thighs like a second skin, making it evident that his legs and buttocks were pure honed muscle.

Were all scholars so fit? The man was built more like a knight than one who spends his time studying scrolls.

She had observed that many Spoltami men dressed in such a way– and it did seem most comfortable– but none looked as he did. Daxan Sahain had a rare quality; Soosha called it the warm, 'stroking-aura'.

When Soosha sensed a man with that quality, she liked to go into his arms and feel them come tight about her. Daxan's *stroking-aura* reminded her of the satisfaction of lazy days spent stretching in the sun– and the perfectly heated passion that was sure to follow.

To a Familiar, this was an extremely desirable trait.

In fact, the quality could cause a female Familiar to turn into a purring mass of 'I will do anything you want'.

So Soosha already ached for him to pet her all night.

She closed her eyes and breathed in the cool, refreshing air of Spoltam. The scents were different from M'yan– but no less enticing.

Above them, the sky had darkened to the deepest purple. Silvery stars skipped across the sky in broad spiraling arcs, twinkling through passing mists of pale lavender clouds. A few bands of pink still remained at the horizon, emphasizing the contrast of the multiple striations.

Truly, it was the most beautiful sunset she had ever seen!

Earlier, the light blue of day sky had slowly feathered

into bands of pink, aqua, lavender, blue– each tint intensifying as night met day.

Later, darker hues entwined with the swirling blushes of pastels. It reminded Soosha of new lovers blending in a caress; their individual beauty merging into a greater sum, a greater brilliance.

Gradually the sky melded into true twilight.

Daxan told her that Aghni was well-known for its extended dusk. "Off-landers often visit solely to witness this splendor."

"I believe it."

Prior to coming to Spoltam, Soosha could not imagine any place as wonderful as M'yan. Yet, in its own way Spoltam was just as resplendent.

Oh, how she wished she could continue to travel! Her heart longed for it. But she was not alone in thinking this; every Familiar on M'yan felt the same way.

Including the King, Gian Ren.

To be safe from slavers, they were forced to make slaves of themselves! For the first time she truly understood the depths of Gian's ruling and the reasons why he had been forced to do it. *Better to choose your own line of control than have others choose for you.*

At least on M'yan they maintained command of their options.

With this new insight Soosha gained the utmost respect for the strength that it must have taken to issue such a proclamation. Gian Ren was truly a great king.

But would M'yan cease being a haven for them? A cage is a cage no matter the size. A constricted Familiar could never be a free Familiar.

Such thoughts depressed her.

Tonight was not a night for such thoughts! This might be the only night she had to convince the man walking beside her that he was meant to be with her forever.

It was much to expect from one eve.

It was much to expect from this man.

If she could not woo him to her way of thinking, she would spend her whole life missing him. Every man's face she saw, every lover she took, would not ease that feeling.

Because Daxan was for her.

If he was Familiar, he would then be subject to the same unhappy fate. Since he was not, she had no way of knowing if he would be affected by her in this deeper way.

Soosha squared her shoulders, ready to take on the seemingly impossible task. Familiar woman could be fierce in many ways.

Some of them obvious and some not so obvious.

Soosha's strength was in seizing the chance. She had always believed that those who sit and say they might have done it, never really knew. She had to *know*.

It would be up to her to make these precious moments with Daxan Sahain count.

The Spoltam sea rushed to the shore in a chortling gurgle of motion. Under the dance of moonrays, the pale green waters were impossibly clear. Laughing, Soosha lifted her skirts to keep them dry as the cool water rushed over her bare feet.

It felt so good to be free!

Daxan grinned at her, his white teeth flashing in the gloaming. "I have always liked the nights in Aghni best. There is an enchanted quality, is there not?"

"Yes! I love it! It is so beautiful!" The sea rushed out again in a gurgling froth of white-aqua spray.

"When I first came to Aghni I spent many a night walking the shoreline. Feeling the still warm sand between my toes, the cool water intermittently greeting me."

Soosha's brow furrowed. "You are not from here?"

"I am not originally from Aghni, no. But my family is an old one and they supported me in my decision to come here."

"Ah, yes. The Spoltami way you have told me about. Are they very far away?"

His lids hooded. "Yes."

"And do you not miss them?"

"I do."

"Then why–"

He reached out and swept a strand of hair off of her cheek. He stared into her eyes. "Because, Soosha, sometimes there is a calling."

Calling? Recently, she had felt a similar feeling. It was why she had left M'yan. "I think I understand."

"It seems these things will come when they will come." The corners of his lips lifted in a self-effacing grin. "I never believed that before. I do now."

Soosha studied the man before her. The man who was to be her mate. He was something of a puzzle. *Had he somehow felt the mating pull?*

No, that was ridiculous.

Unless. . . Spoltami could also sense their mates.

"Do you– how do Spoltami mate?" The question was blurted out before Soosha had a chance to think of how odd it might sound.

Caught off guard by her blunt inquiry, Daxan gave her a peculiar look. "I am not sure what you are asking me, sweet adventurer." His golden hair lifted past his shoulders with the breeze as he tried to figure out her question.

Soosha stuck her big toe in a clump of wet sand and flung the moist little load directly onto the arch of his foot. "I am asking if your people. . . you know. . . *mate*."

Daxan was a master at deciphering reactions. Often words alone were not enough to tell the entire tale. She had flung the sand at the arch of his foot for a reason.

His returning smile was a slow, sensual one. "We mate all the time," he replied. "Sometimes several times in one night."

Soosha snorted. "No. I mean a permanent mating. Is that the custom here?"

"Not always. We sometimes have a series of various connections."

Her brow furrowed. "How long do these connections last?"

"As long as the people who are involved wish them to last."

Soosha wondered if he was referring to play partners. That concept was not foreign to her. Familiars often enjoyed many partners before they mated. However, once mated, they engaged with their mates and no other.

Soosha was not sure she understood the Spoltam way.

As they passed a red spiky plant, Daxan snapped off a thin stalk and placed it between his lips.

Soosha smiled to herself. Worlds apart, yet males still liked to play with blades of plants!

He glanced at her out of the corner of his eye. "What is mating like where you are from?"

Soosha had a dilemma.

She had no doubt that her older brother would be showing up soon to drag her home. Brygar was just *that* way.

What was more he was sure to cause a ruckus; the man

always roared first and purred later. She bit her lip as she played out the coming spectacle in her mind. By Aiyah, it would not be pleasant!

Sometimes Brygar needed to be scratched for his own good.

She loved her brother but he was an intractable handful of stubborn male! He was a huge Familiar with jet black hair and the unusual combination of pale lavender/ pale aqua eyes. In his cat form he looked exactly the way one might imagine; and he considered whatever household he entered, *owned*.

To say he would make her situation difficult would be an understatement.

Chances were that even if by some miracle Daxan accepted their mating situation, he would not readily accept her impossible brother.

She was confident that would change, given enough time. Brygar was a potent force to deal with, but everyone eventually came to love him.

Or at least put up with him for short periods of time.

And as lovely as this planet was to look at, she was not at all enamored of its society. Surely even a Spoltami mate would understand and agree with that viewpoint?

After all, she was the female and he must please her!

That was what the women of M'yan expected. . . *and always got.* It was unthinkable not to have an impossible sense of entitlement!

The idea that Daxan would not want to leave his home never took hold in her mind. He *would* come with her.

On the other hand, until the man was ready to do so, she could not simply grab a hank of his golden beaded hair and drag him back to M'yan.

Although the idea did hold great appeal.

He was a comely male.

Unfortunately, she was working without a guide; it was not as if females of her species chose non-Familiars mates every day! Soosha had to figure out how to go about actually joining with him.

Perhaps, she should begin by enticing him into partaking of a few of their rituals?

Yes, then part of her problem would be solved!

He was still waiting for her answer about Familiar mating. She did not want to scare him away by telling him that they were to be mated; however, if she did this carefully, he could act out the ritual for himself.

"We do not speak of our mating to anyone. It is a personal matter for Familiar alone."

"Now you have made me curious."

That was good. "Mmm. As a scholar, I imagine you would have great interest in the process?"

"Indeed I do." He paused. "Strictly as a scholar, mind you."

That was bad. Soosha's shoulders slumped.

Daxan scratched his jaw as he watched her through lowered lids. "I have heard the act is shrouded in secrecy. Rumors abound. Some say you Familiar mate for *days* on end. There are those who fantasize what that could possibly entail. . . if it is true?"

Soosha perked up. *Now we are getting somewhere, Daxan Sahain!* She eagerly leaned forward.

Too eagerly.

Seemingly embarrassed, he cleared his throat noisily. "I am not one of them, of course."

"Of course." She mentally threw her hands up in the air.

This was impossible! A Familiar man would have already been pressed behind her! Hot. Hard.

And ready.

Growling into her throat as he showed her just why he was the man chosen for her. . .

Yes, a Familiar man would already be licking her from her nape to the back of her heels!

And that would simply be his introductory greeting. His full introduction might be a week in the making.

Soosha flattened her lips into what was definitely a frustrated grimace.

Daxan gave her a sidelong look. "Yet, I would like to know more, Soosha. Can you not tell me anything?"

At last. "Like so many things, it depends upon our mood..."

"Spoken like a true feline." His dimpled grin was truly engaging. And altogether seductive.

"But who leads the dance here?" she mumbled.

"Hmm?" He blinked slowly, spiky black lashes fanning beautiful golden eyes. *Secretive* golden eyes.

"Which one is your dwelling?" Soosha scanned the top of the cliff wall. Large estates dotted the rocky promontory.

Daxan came up behind her, placing his large hands firmly on her shoulders. He pivoted her position slightly, then pulled her back, close against him.

Very close.

Soosha could feel the pulsing heat of him right through the thin gown she was wearing. A brisk, wonderful scent emanated from his tunic. The fragrance hit her like the waves hit the shore. Forceful. Exotic. Lush. It evoked sea winds and enigmatic, faraway places.

His servants must wash his raiment in Spoltam spices.

The aromatic fragrance was spellbinding! She would have to bring some back to M'yan with her. "What is this wondrous scent in your clothing, Daxan?"

He shifted his focus from the cliffs to glance lazily down at her. His perfectly shaped mouth parted slightly and his eyes seemed to cloud over. "Do you like it?" His voice rolled in his throat with a husky ripple.

"*Oh, yes*. I would like to purchase a large quantity in your *sacri* to bring back with me."

"Would you?" His low chuckle reverberated against her back. The warm breath that followed skittered along her nape, enervating the nerve endings.

Strange, but his stance almost mirrored her earlier thoughts; he was right behind her, just as she had fantasized. "Why do you find my request so humorous? Do these spiced oils have some hidden meaning for your people?"

"Shhh."

Unwittingly, she did shut her eyes as he spoke softly in her ear– *in that husky voice*. The low tone sent scalding chills through her. "Do you see that small dwelling next to the outcropping?"

"Y-yes." She eased back against him.

"I can purchase some scents there for you but I do not think they will match; I am told mine is a special blend."

She was disappointed. If she could not replicate the same scent, she was not particularly interested. "Oh. Never mind, then. I thank you anyway."

"Soosha, I am willing to give you as much of my fragrance as you desire."

"But. . . I would not want to take this special blend from you, Daxan."

"You need but ask and it is yours. Whenever you want. To return the favor, perhaps you can tell me something about this mating ritual you Familiar have. . ."

Are his lips nibbling my throat? Soosha blinked. The touch was so gentle, so perfect, she unconsciously purred. "Ah, I see; you are teasing me for the sake of your knowledge."

"I am teasing you?" His deep voice was hoarse. "Are you sure that is the way it is?" A warm mouth slid down the back of her neck, sending chills of desire up her spine.

It appeared her Spoltami was able to carry certain things along just fine.

Yet there was a delicious torment to this slow game she played. Female Familiars took great pleasure in making their males *work* for their attention.

The feline in her did not want to make it too easy for him.

A small mew-like sound, only made by female Familiars and their cat-selves, issued her lips. It was a cross between a sigh and a cry.

The small utterance signified a myriad of emotions which roughly boiled down to: *'We know we are going to end up doing this but I am certainly not going to let you know I know it.'*

The unconscious utterance made Daxan's lips widen into a grin against the back of her neck. His sweet breath teased at her sensitized skin.

Strange, but her body already recognized this man. Recognized and wanted him.

It all came down to him. Every caress she was seeking. Every kiss her lips craved. Every stroke of touch.

The thrusts of his body that she ached to feel. . .

For a Familiar the mating moment was perfectly clear. All others did not matter.

It would only ever be Daxan.

Soosha was so curious about him! She wanted to know everything. She longed to explore his layers.

Yet, there was one question that plagued her above all others. How did she know he was to be her mate when she had not been triggered by the male response first?

Was there something about Spoltami males that triggered the response? If so what did it mean?

Daxan's open mouth slid over her shoulder, a hint of teeth scraping the apex of the curve.

Soosha sucked in her breath. That particular spot was a very sensitive one for a Familiar woman. *Did he somehow know that or was it happenstance?*

Probably a coincidence.

Or a fortunate deed.

Or. . . perhaps, Spoltami men were very interesting indeed.

"Tell me, what is wrong with a passion for knowledge, my beautiful Familiar?"

"The pursuit of knowledge to the exclusion of all else can blind one to life's true passions. "

"Do you think I am imperceptive?" He laved the skin behind her ear with a light flick of his tongue. Then he gave her the tiniest of bites on the very rim of her lobe.

She shivered. "I have not yet decided what you are."

"We all hold mysteries. I do not 'explain' myself to anyone."

"Never say that to a Familiar. We are curious by nature and your words lure me into finding out more about you."

He chuckled. "I look forward to the attempt."

Although Daxan leveled out his breathing, hot puffs of air feathered her skin as his pulse rate increased. Before she knew it, strong arms were around her, pulling her tight up against him.

Well, Spoltami men hide treasure beneath their tunics. The hefty stone-like bulge that pressed against her buttocks left no doubt of that. Apparently a cool scholar could burn like fire when passion took control of his mind.

Interesting.

"You must be hungry," he whispered.

Oh yes, she was. Only not for food.

Soosha took a deep breath. She had to steady herself! Remember that he was different; that his ways were different. This act must done in a specific manner.

And not as a fast coupling, either.

What she had in mind was hours upon hours of unrelenting passion.

The poor man had no idea what was in store for him.

Taking another deep breath, she forced herself to a calmer state. It was not easy; she was wet with desire. Briefly she wondered if she could take him quickly at first, here on the beach under the stars. . .

No!

Not with him. Not the first time.

The first time they came together must be in the traditional Familiar mating stance!

So. . . how was she to get him to do that?

There had to be a way!

"This is a good spot."

At first she thought he meant on her throat, but then realized he had thrown the vine basket onto a nearby outcropping of rock that jutted out into the water.

Nimbly jumping onto the rocky ledge, Daxan held his hand out for her. "Lift your skirts to make the jump. I believe you will like it up here."

As she reached out for his hand, she noticed a bronze cuff on his forearm just below the elbow. Stretched taut over his skin, the cuff complimented his golden skin, accentuating the sinews and carved muscles of his arm.

The intricate armband was woven with hundreds of thin metallic threads! The complex pattern reminded Soosha of the patterns that Aviaran men wove with ribbons into their wives' hair.

She wondered if the adornment had any significance other than ornamental?

Probably an ancient Spoltam warning regarding their large speckled fruit.

Her nose twitched as she thought about it.

After helping her up onto the ledge, Daxan sat down and sifted through the vine basket.

Soosha took the opportunity to examine the rocky promontory they were on, noting that a partial wall to her right effectively blocked some of the wind, as well as the houses on the high cliff. Down below, the Spoltam sea frothed onto pink sand; above her, the crisp night sky winked with sparkling stars that seemed to have countless stories to tell!

The secluded place Daxan had chosen was utterly intoxicating.

All of her senses were responding to its charm.

The location could not be more perfect for what she had in mind. The wind would ignite Daxan's passion, the rolling sea would cover his cries of ecstasy.

"We can have our feast here." Daxan was staring at her,

not the food. And the sensual tone of his voice suggested that he also had a different kind of sustenance in mind.

Which was good.

He had finally given her the perfect means to carry out a proper Familiar mating.

Familiars always put high value on the physical. Like others of her kind, Soosha believed that intimacy should always come first, so that whatever remained could follow naturally. For Soosha, mated lovemaking was a spiritual awakening, a closeness, and a renewal that could only come about through the sexual act.

As Soosha thought about the intimacies she would soon be sharing with this handsome man– who was all but a stranger– a flush rose to her cheeks and her aqua and gold eyes dilated with desire.

Daxan smiled slowly. He had no trouble reading her expression. Grabbing a small pouch from the vine basket, he rose from his seat to stand next to her.

He handed her a small leather covered bottle. "Try this; I think you will like it."

Soosha opened the flask and took an experimental, wary sniff. Most Familiars were very particular about what they consumed. They never took anyone's word for how good it was; they had to sniff for themselves first.

The cautious trait was deeply ingrained in their makeup.

Probably for good reason.

It took a hunter to know that there was always the thinnest of lines between hunter and hunted. Situations could turn quickly.

"What is it?" she asked warily.

"An elixir made from a large, speckled Spoltam fruit. It is called *Nightfall*. The drink is very popular with both

Spoltami and visitors, alike. You will find it served in all of the taverns here."

Soosha sniffed at the *Nightfall* again. It could not be made from that awful-smelling fruit! It could not. The scent had changed into something utterly alluring. "Um, what does it taste like?"

"Indescribable. You will have to find out for yourself." He held the vial up to her lips. "Drink."

She cautiously took a sip. The spicy blend was somewhat thick; it slid down her throat in a smooth wash. "Mmmm, that was quite re–"

Her eyes opened wide as the elixir bounded back with a strong punch. "*Oh!*"

He laughed at her reaction. "I should have warned you––it has tooth."

"There is nothing wrong with a little teeth," she purred seductively, licking a droplet off her lips. "Every now and then," she whispered. The tip of her pink tongue delicately dabbed at the sweet spot.

Daxan watched her through the lowered veil of his lashes. "So you like some bite. . . occasionally?" he murmured drily.

"At the right time, it can be the perfect stimulant." She gave him a guileless look– as if they had only been discussing the elixir. "Do you export it? I would love to bring such an exotic taste home with me." Oh, she was being quite naughty!

But Soosha could not help herself. She was true to her feline sisters!

"First, you want my fragrance," his voice was a husky whisper, "Then my *Nightfall*. I best be careful what else I introduce you to, Soosha. It seems you want to take everything home with you."

She smiled secretively. "We familiar do like to carry the odd prize back every now and again."

"So I have heard." Daxan rested back against the rock wall. "To answer your question, we do not export our Nightfall. There is a rumor that the potency does not last long once it is produced; so it must be imbibed within an evening. This means this very potent brew must be consumed at the one time. That makes it a popular tavern choice. Off-Landers think fondly of us by remembering the experience and, thus, come more often to visit. " He gave her a wink as he raised the bottle to his lips. "Good for profits, you see."

She tapped the side of her forehead with her index finger. "Smart Spoltami."

"We are a clever people." He took a healthy swig of the strong drink.

"But are you wise?"

He swirled the bottle in his hand as he mulled over her question. "*That* is a complex question. Do you think we are wise?"

"I do not know. It seems to me in some things, perhaps. Yet, there might be room for more studying." She gave him a gamin grin.

"Wisely put, my Familiar friend."

"You agree with me?" This surprised her; he seemed to have such a high regard for his people's level of knowledge.

Daxan rubbed the back of his neck under the heavy fall of his hair. Soosha thought his gesture very sensual. "I suppose Spoltam is not as perfect as we would like to believe."

That was an subtle statement if she ever heard one. "It is very different from my home planet."

"I suspect it is."

"Perhaps one day you would like to see our M'yan?" She watched him, expectantly. Few were issued such an invitation; M'yan was a protected haven.

His golden eyes locked with hers. "I would love to visit your world." His hand reached up and cupped the side of her face. "They say it is intoxicating. . . Like its people."

Soosha sighed wistfully and looked down. Just thinking about her beautiful home made her miss it.

Raising her eyes to his, she suddenly became aware of the way he was staring at her. *Like he wanted to drink her until he drowned.*

"Yes," she breathed. "Intoxicating."

Daxan placed the elixir vial on the rocky ledge behind her. His free arm smoothly encircled her waist, bringing her to him. He watched her. Silently. Mysteriously.

The wind gently ruffled his hair. Silvery moonlight reflected off of lambent golden eyes.

What is he thinking behind those amber shields?

Soosha realized his features were not defined by perfection, but by angular strokes of masculine synergy.

He was capturing her.

Daxan Sahain, you are most compelling.

Right then and there, she decided to do away with the preliminaries. "I would like to make love to you."

"I know."

There was that slightly wicked tilt to the edges of his lips. The man was matching her step for step!

She arched her brow. "Perhaps Spoltam men are wiser than I have given them credit for after all?"

"I would not judge most Spoltami by me, my honeyed savager of market stalls."

Her lips curled into a grin. His apt description of the frantic chase through the Spoltam *sacri* made her laugh.

He laughed with her.

Bending his head close to hers, he hugged her in his arms. Daxan's *stroke-aura* was just as she imagined; only better. It was like being embraced by rays of sunlight. Warm, appeasing, purrrr-fect.

His sweet breath, laden with the spices of *Nightfall*, caressed her lips. His mouth–that delectable, firm mouth–was so close!

Yet their lips did not touch.

It was said on M'yan that a male's true skill in the art of pleasure was to be found in the "tips". Of his tongue. Of his fingers. Of his member.

As a general rule, Soosha believed the adage undoubtedly true. But there was much to be said for other skills.

Anticipation was also an art.

As Daxan stared deeply into her eyes, his measured exhales teasing at her mouth, Soosha instinctively knew that he was a man who could wield anticipation with the deadly precision of a Charl lightblade.

He *was* playing with her.

And she rather liked it.

Daxan brought her closer, clasping her to him. His fingers splayed across the sleek cloth of her gown. The *tips* of his fingers pressed into her flesh as he slowly caressed the material over her smooth thighs and buttocks.

Clenching his fist, Daxan easily lifted the gown. The cool night air kissed her stroke-warmed skin.

His bare arm pressed into her bare thigh, the flat of his hands gliding across her buttocks in a smooth caress. Back and forth– he massaged the soft material against her skin, bunching it in his fists; his knuckles strumming the curve of a rounded cheek. . .

Then his nails skittered down the back of her thigh. Scoring just enough to tingle and not scratch. Teasingly, he pressed his face into the side of her neck.

Soosha's breath caught in her throat. *What was he doing*? Would he actually *bite* her?

Still not touching her with his lips, Daxan inhaled her scent, then blew a steady stream of cool air along her collarbone.

Tiny bumps of anticipation rose up on her skin.

Gathering her gown in both hands, Daxan repeated his actions, bunching the material, massaging her with the silken cloth, rubbing it against her flushed skin, and finally, alternating his motions with the tips of his fingers, bringing bare skin in contact with bare skin.

The hardened *tips* of Soosha's breasts jutted against the thin cloth of the gown.

Daxan dipped his head. His hands cupped her buttocks with the bunched cloth; the *tips* of his coiled , beaded hair teased across those sensitized nubs, sliding back and forth.

Then, suddenly his mouth was there.

Scalding directly through the fabric, fastening on the pebbled crest. He suckled with strength and he was not gentle.

Soosha's reaction was so intense that she jumped in his arms.

Daxan murmured low in his throat. The rumble of satisfaction reminded Soosha of male pleasure-purring.

How she loved *that* sound!

Soon the cloth became moistened from his mouth, sticking to her breasts. When he removed his pliant lips, the wet spot became instantly cooled from the night breeze.

He blew hot breath across the jutting peak.

The feeling was exquisite! Soosha moaned as she opened her senses to experience every sensation.

He repeated his ministrations to her other breast.

Drawing on the firm peak through the silky cloth, he exhaled a scorching wave of breath, following up on the action with a cool stream of air. All the while his hands massaged and caressed her buttocks and upper thighs.

Oh, he was good. *So good.*

Agilely, he dropped to his knees before her.

His open mouth slid down the center line of her midriff, over her stomach directly to the juncture between her legs. Daxan was so smooth, his actions so fluid, that Soosha acquired a new appreciation of the Spoltam male.

She was soon to 'appreciate' him even more.

Palms flattened against her buttocks, he drew her right against his mouth. He had her trapped in a scalding love embrace that allowed no room for escape. Soosha's nails dug into his shoulders.

He *was* surprising her!

The tip of his tongue flicked the centerline of her nether lips, softly stabbing at the fabric. *Scalding hot*. His tongue slipped between the covered folds, tasting her 'nightfall' as it seeped right through the material.

Daxan made Soosha flow and flow and the cloth became drenched with her dewy moisture.

His white teeth pulled the material taut over her mound– adding just the *right* pressure. Trapped by his

114

hands, Soosha thrashed beneath his mouth and almost clawed at his back.

A wave crested the lower edge of the rocky promontory and a spray of cool sea water sluiced over them both.

Daxan's shoulders and back were drenched and the water dripped off of him directly onto her nether lips. Soosha was burning and shivering at the same time. Wet *and wet*.

Daxan was just hot.

His tongue flicked into her folds– but he did not touch the one place that throbbed and ached for his touch!

His fingernails scored the back of her thighs exactly as the edge of his teeth scraped against the cleft of her mound.

He suckled her then. Strong. And he was not gentle.

Soosha arched up, moaning; she cried out words in the secret Familiar tongue that she was glad he could not understand. She spoke of his expert touch; the sleek, perfect way he moved his mouth on her; and of how much she wanted him inside her . . . She told him he could lead this first dance– because he must; but she also warned him that she would be coming for him in every way. . . She begged for her release, then she *demanded* it. . . . She promised him he would soon tremble for her.

Soosha's fingers clasped Daxan's shoulders, and she could feel the Spoltami man *shaking* with desire.

He briefly paused to stare up at her through a thick crescent of ebony lashes. Again, that low sound rumbled in his chest. His golden eyes glittered with an almost *wild* intent.

Daxan's inflamed reaction gave her pause.

Had she misjudged the men of Spoltam? What if their cool, scholarly exteriors hid something raw beneath the surface? Come to think on it. . . what did she actually know of these people?

Nothing.

Soosha swallowed nervously.

"Um. . . are your people. . ."

But she never got to finish her question.

Daxan drew up the edge of her gown and before she could even move his mouth was directly on her. Devouring her with unbridled passion.

Soosha threw back her head, crying out with ecstasy at the incredible sensation!

"I see there are elixirs even more potent and more rare than Nightfall," he whispered hoarsely, the vibration of his deep voice making her quiver.

Right then, he mastered her with his lips and mouth.

Dipping his tongue inside her, Daxan drank of her elixir as if he could not taste enough . He flicked and laved and suckled until Soosha could take no more.

She arched up on the tips of her toes; and throwing back her head, she screamed her release to the sea and the sky.

Daxan did not stop.

Even as she poured over him, peaking again and again, he did not stop.

She became dizzy with it; but he kept getting more and more of her, bringing her to impossible heights. He knew exactly how much she could give and, until he was sure she had given it *to him*, he would not cease.

Only when she sagged against him, utterly spent, did he relent.

He caught her with one arm as he stood, tugging the gown over her head in one fluid motion.

Still holding her, he tossed his own tunic and breeches

116

aside as well. Then he rested back against the wall of stones, holding her in his arms; clasped tight to his hot, naked skin.

The cuffed armband– his only adornment now– made its presence felt with a cool slide under her breasts. His erect manhood jutted betwixt her thighs; the hard rod seemed as if it was encloaked in the finest *krilli*. Silky smooth.

Soosha's eyelids fluttered open, the pupils still hazy from spent passion.

Daxan cupped her face. His strong fingers threaded her hair; sifting through the wondrous length. "It is true, is it not?" He drawled; his voice rough with desire.

"Wh-what is true?" Soosha was still trying to catch her breath.

"The rumor that Familiar women have a special taste all their own? A nectar that can drive any man wild."

Soosha's face flamed. "I would not know."

Daxan gave her an odd look. "You–"

"I have only been with my kind, Daxan; and they seem to like us well enough." She blushed. "This is my first journey off M'yan. Our men do not like us to travel unprotected."

He seemed to think about that. "I can understand why. You put yourself at great risk, Soosha."

She shrugged philosophically. "Life is a risk."

"True, but there are many kinds of risk. Will you now tell me how Familiars mate? If you will but share a small portion of this knowledge with me, I vow I will not tell anyone."

Soosha bit her lip. "Is it just for the knowledge, then?"

He shook his head. "No. I want to experience some of the intensity of this passion as well. It is something that I have felt calling to me. . . Something I think I have been missing. Sometimes knowledge is not enough; we need passion to fire our quest for learning."

This she could understand. Though she doubted he *truly* did.

Of course she would share the knowledge with him.

She was meant to.

His asking had made the task that much easier. She only hoped he would still understand when all was said and done.

"Very well. I shall share our customs with you."

His smoky gaze was so complacent, that it almost gave her pause.

She glanced down the length of him. His nude body was male perfection. Perfectly proportioned muscles and sinews honed to the peak of flawlessness.

He was so beautiful that he could match any male on her world.

Undoubtedly, there were things that Spoltam males did that she could learn and experience. "Daxan, perhaps later you will share the Spoltami way with me?"

The smile that shaped his lips was close to being predatory. His finger lifted her chin, forcing her to look up at him. "Do you think you are ready to accept this new knowledge, sweet adventurer?"

Soosha bristled at the question, squaring her shoulders. "Is this not why I have come here, after all?"

As soon as she said it, Soosha realized that it *was* the reason she had come to Spoltam. Her journey here had not been an accident. Spoltam had called to her because her mating had called to her.

If she had stayed on M'yan and followed Gian's wishes, she would not have found Daxan.

But would the King listen to that justification when the time came to go before him and answer for what she had done?

"Then you begin, my lady visitor." Daxan accepted her words and opened the way for her.

"Very well. First, we Familiar like to commence with a. . . um. . . a. . . declaration of. . . of-" She was not sure how to say this.

"Of the sensual promises you are going to deliver?" he supplied helpfully.

"Exactly."

He motioned with his hand. "Proceed."

"Fine. Um, since you have no knowledge of the secret Familiar tongue you will not understand the phrases . . ."

"I am hoping your actions will be all the translation I need," he drawled.

Soosha colored. "They will," she promised. He had no idea that in Familiar society it was the male that did the taking and the promising.

Which suited their females just fine.

It was not easy to round up a male Familiar. Once their vows were made; they could not be broken.

"Now repeat after me. 'Daxan Sahain K'tea'." She spoke the oath in her mind as well. *This Familiar takes you.*

"Daxan Sa'ain K'tea." he repeated after her.

"Ei mahana ne Tuan." she continued. *And discards all others.*

"Daxan Sa'ain K'mea sut la." *This Familiar will give himself only to you .*

"Ei ra Tuan." *And no other.*

"Daxan Sa'ain litna K'shintauk rehan." *This Familiar unites with you now forever.*

"A jhan vri re Tuan." *For him there is no other.*

While he spoke the words, he closed his eyes as if he were trying to put meaning to them.

When he finished speaking, he opened them. The golden orbs were clouded over.

"Now what do we do?" he whispered huskily. His breaths were slow and methodical, as if he were purposely holding himself back.

But that did not make sense.

Holding himself back from what?

Soosha hesitated. Normally, this was the part of the ceremony where the male would seize his mate's breath in a kiss of searing possession. He would take her breath inside him, making it his, combining it with his own, blending them as one.

Then he would return his breath to her; and her breath would be his, always.

Truly, it was not a favorite part of the ceremony for the female.

Most struggled against it.

It suddenly donned on Soosha that Daxan would not be able to complete the last part of the ceremony! Why had she not thought of that before? What was she to do now?

Mayhap in this situation, his oath would be sufficient?

She had never found out what Krue and Suleila had done, so she had no idea. Knowing Krue though, he had probably taken Suleila to wife under Charl mystical law.

"Well?"

"Um. . . You must now act out your words."

His deep voice rolled off his tongue. "I am willing. How do I do that?"

"You must stand behind me-"

Daxan grinned slowly. Sensually. "I am liking this already." He moved behind her as she faced the rock wall. "The view is certainly spectacular." He pinched her buttock.

Soosha gasped and jumped at the same time. "Be serious, Daxan Sahain! I am showing you a time-honored ritual!"

"Of course. My apologies. Please continue."

"Well, now you must. . .that is, we prefer. . .um. . . ."

"I think I already did that." He grinned.

"You are not amusing, you know."

"Mmmm. Perhaps I missed the *translation*."

Soosha ignored his teasing. This was not so easy to instruct as she had thought. She had never realized how odd their customs were until they had to be taught to someone. *Out loud.*

"I. . .um. . .ah. . .well, you have to. . .ah. . ."

"Are you trying to tell me to enter you from behind?" Daxan's wry tone did not help.

"I. . .well. . ." Soosha flushed. "There is a bit more to it than that."

"Really? I would not have thought so."

She heard the smile in his words. "This is serious! Do not make sport of me."

"I would not."

But she knew the Spoltami was highly amused. How did she tell this scholar the next part? He would flee back to his stone house and slam the doors tight!

"What else is there, *my kitten*?"

"When you are ready to. . .to. . .proceed, you must, well, bite the back of my neck at the same time you come inside."

A cough burst out of his mouth. *"Bite the back of your neck?"* His voice sounded aghast, but behind her, he looked up at the sky, dimples curving his cheeks. "What do you mean? You want me to simply nibble lightly along your throat?"

"No! I mean the male must sharply bite, well, actually, clamp his teeth–"

This was extremely awkward.

The ritual sounded entirely strange when spoken aloud in such a manner. What would he think of her people? They would seem savage to him!

"Let us forget this. I see it is not a good idea." She made to move away.

"Oh, I think it is an excellent idea." He quickly pressed against her from behind, nudging her thighs apart. Capturing her within his hold.

Apparently his swollen shaft thought it was a excellent idea as well; a droplet of moisture trickled onto the curve of her buttock.

The man was aroused; but would he actually be able to perform the traditional mating?

"Daxan, I do not think you fully understa–"

"I believe I can get the way of it, Soosha." He whispered softly into her ear as he swept her hair to one side, over her shoulder.

Before she could say anything else, he entwined his fingers with hers and stretched his arm out against the rock wall. The *tip* of his shaft teased the crevice of her buttocks. The *tip* of his tongue swirled around the folds of her ear.

His moist breath was hot on the back of her neck. It sent shivers of desire through her.

"Now you probably should-"

Instead of waiting for further instructions, Daxan Sahain

did *exactly* as he was meant to do; he sharply bit the back of her neck and thrust into her in one swift, powerful stroke that would have done any male Familiar proud.

"*Daxan!*"

"Mmmmmm-hmmmm." His hot mouth swept along her throat, kissing and nipping as he held her fast in the mating embrace.

There, he remained imbedded in her, standing firm and marking his time. His uneven, rough breaths cascaded over her back like warm sand clouds.

Behind them, the moon rose high in the evening sky. The rays of light silhouetted them against the rocks, locked in the age-old Familiar joining stance.

"N'taga," Soosha breathed. *You have placed your shadow on me.*

Daxan whispered raggedly in her ear. "Look, Soosha, our shadows are blending on the rock face."

"Yes, I see them. We Familiar have a name for it; we call it Shadow Dance. It is. . . well, it is something special to us."

"*Soosha.*"

"What is it, Daxan?" She started to turn but he began sliding in her. Long strokes, deep.

Soosha groaned and purred at the same time. "Do- do you need me to tell you what to do next?"

"Not unless you wish to." He grinned and nipped her shoulder.

Releasing her hands, he caught at the locks of her hair and unclasped one of the long strands of Aghni pearls. He tossed the long tresses over his own shoulders. The silken mass glided down his naked back, causing him to moan. It felt even better than he remembered.

His hips ground into her with a circular motion as he looped the pearl strand around both of their waists, and then threaded it through her legs.

"What do you do with the pearls in-"

"You will see."

And see, she did.

He lashed the ends of the cording around his wrists. With every thrust, he drew the pearls over the front of her mound, tugging them one by one across her nether lips.

Soosha threw back her head and cried out with the exquisite torture. She had no idea how inventive Spoltami males were!

Daxan continually changed the tempo of his strokes, from long measured thrusts to faster tugs of the pearls. When he suddenly *flexed* sharply inside her, Soosha tumbled over the edge yet again.

But this time he felt the contractions all along the length of his embedded member. They captured him in the most sensual embrace of all.

His voice became as raw as his passion. "As you are bound by these pearls, Soosha, so, too, am I."

She thought he referred to the manner in which he had wrapped them together. It was inspired; he had cleverly bound them in such a way as to wring the utmost pleasure out of the situation. Every time she moved, the strand did to him what he was doing to her.

Daxan groaned as she suddenly tightened her thighs on him. Still keeping hold of the pearls, he grabbed the vial of *NightFall*. Instead of drinking it, he poured it over her breasts. The thick, tangy juice flowed to the peaks of her breasts and dripped off the tips.

He massaged the elixir into the rosy skin with his

palms.

The rubbing action intermittently pulled the pearl strand taut against them both, adding to their mutual pleasure. All the while, he moved in her, never relinquishing his steady tempo.

Immediately, the *Nightfall* began to sizzle her nerve endings. Her breasts throbbed with unbearable pressure!

As if he knew how heightened her senses were becoming, Daxan looped the pearls around the tips of her breasts and gently drew the strand back and forth.

The pearls hit her in seven pleasure points at once.

Soosha's breath choked in her throat.

Daxan cupped her breasts in his palms and roughly flicked her nipples with his thumbs.

Again the man had her rearing up on her toes as he indulged her pleasure. The waves tumbled rapidly over one another as she peaked in his arms.

But Daxan Sahain was not finished yet.

Picking up the *Nightfall* once again, he splashed some into his cupped palms. Soosha had an idea what he planned to do.

She also had an idea that *Nightfall* was more than just a Spoltami liquor. Her mate had brought a pleasure potion along with their meal. Very intriguing. . .

Even though she had been expecting it, when he cupped his hand over her mound to let the rich elixir seep against her, she was not prepared for the devastating effect. *The Nightfall burned its way into her, setting off explosion after explosion!*

It was as if she throbbed everywhere!

It was too much even for a Familiar woman. Soosha screamed and scratched at him as peak after peak came to her– and yet she wanted more of the feeling. More of him.

Daxan clasped her hips tightly, and began to thrust in earnest. Swiftly and powerfully. As he stroked, some of the burning *Nightfall* juices rode with him into her canal, instantly inflaming them both– almost unendurably.

Another spray of sea water crested the cliff, drenching them in a cool slap of water.

It was good that they were in a secluded spot for they both yelled out their ecstasy.

Daxan became wild as the *Nightfall* mixed with Soosha's own, distinctive moisture. The normal effect of the female Familiar's secretions seemed to treble and his released passion turned feral.

He could hold back no longer.

Daxan bit her shoulder and flipped them both around so he was slanting back against the stone wall and she faced forward while they stood. His palms at the sides of her waist moved her up and down. He guided her onto his shaft, then maneuvered her to ride him in this rather unusual way.

It was an inspired position. Soosha was surprised by his clever resourcefulness. Her buttocks pressed against his groin and, in turn, he pressed into her in ways that allowed a surfeit of new sensations.

He was sexually creative.

Moreover, the Spotami male did not seem to be tiring in the least! In fact, Daxan came to his first peak, crossed over it with clenched teeth and a husky tremor of satisfaction, and kept on going.

Soosha could not have been happier.

The males of Spoltam gained much respect from her. Mayhap she would not have to hold herself back this eve?

Her Spoltami scholar was keeping up with her sigh for sigh.

And so he did for the entire night.

On the rocks. Off the rocks. As the sea crashed into the shore. As the stars flickered through the sea mist. They took each other in a turbulent exchange and their wild cries mixed with the Aghni night.

. By the time Daxan carried Soosha back to his dwelling on the cliffside, most of his beaded hair coils had come undone and his armband had long since been ripped off in the throes of passion.

Marveling at their uninhibited encounter, he tossed the cuff into the Zot vine basket, and looped it over his wrist. Then he scooped a listless Soosha into his arms.

Albeit pleasing, dawn in Aghni was nowhere near as spectacular as the dusk. Yet to Daxan Sahain, a man who had just spent the night exploring Familiar sensuality, this daybreak was the most spectacular he had ever seen.

He brought Soosha to his chamber, securely deposited her in his enormous bed, climbed in beside her, and fell into an exhausted sleep.

Nestled with her safe in his arms– cozy between the krilli coverlet and the soft, fluffy bedding– Daxan's sated slumber was pure bliss.

Soosha awoke to the pleasant sensation of a male pressing solidly against her.

She smiled. So Daxan Sahain liked to cuddle?

Another surprise.

Last night, his lovemaking had been erotic and supremely fulfilling. For a man who was not Familiar, he was very, very inventive.

There was *something* in the way he touched her. . .

In the way he took her.

Something she could not identify.

Muted light streaked through the room from the open balcony doors. The sun already traveled low in the sky; it was well past midday. Soosha could tell by the cadence of Daxan's breathing that he was waking up.

With that realization came an unaccountable shyness.

Soosha was suddenly not sure what she would say to the man. Last night they had both become wild. Would the scholar regret his uninhibited actions in the light of day?

Worse, what would he say when he found out she had actually mated him? *Good morrow, Soosha, you have such a witty sense of humor?* By Aiyah, she did not think he would say that.

The covers rustled and there he was– leaning over her with a lazy, sated smile on his handsome face.

Daxan's long hair had come completely undone. The mass spread across his naked shoulders in a glorious swath of amber.

The tousled strands flowed like liquid gold!

Freed now from the confines of the beaded coils, his hair revealed its true complexity– not one shade of color. . . *but thousands.*

The myriad tones interwove every strand like gilded bands of molten sunlight.

Hair like that should never be confined, she immediately concluded. The style he normally wore, although attractive, concealed its radiant beauty.

Soosha could not stop staring at it.

Truly, his hair was extraordinary for a–

The oddest sensation seeped into her. Warily, she glanced up at his features.

Two different colored eyes glinted down at her.

Soosha's breathing stopped. One eye was sea green, the other sun gold! She could not believe it– He was a Familiar!

And a stunningly beautiful one at that.

"You-you tricked me, Daxan Sahain!"

"Yes."

"Why?"

He gave her with a very catlike smile. {*"Why do you*

think?} He mouthed the words silently as he sent the thought to her mind.

An alluring scent immediately covered her. It was the same enthralling fragrance she had mistaken earlier for Aghni spices in his clothing. Her nostrils flared as she remembered his words: *'I am told mine is a special blend...''*

It was special; true enough. It was the seductive scent of a male Familiar!

Soosha pursed her lips in anger. Oh, he had not lied; there was simply another meaning to his words! Yes, he was one of their males, all right! Cunning. Artful. *Dangerous.*

He had hid himself so well. A true hunter, to be sure. Oh, but he had deceived her in every way!

Her heart sank. Who was he really? Did she even know his true name? And why was he on Spoltam, when all Familiar were recalled to M'yan? Was he a male who had gone feral?

Soosha swallowed. As a young girl she had heard terrifying stories of such males; they were a wild breed. Unconditionally wild. She had heard warnings: if she should have the misfortune to cross one she should never let her guard down. Never.

Soosha needed to get away from him before he truly sealed their fate! He *had* triggered her mating response!

At the moment, the only thing she could think of to do was bolt. She began to struggle in his embrace.

Daxan held her fast.

As he examined her features, she easily recognised the low, rumbling sounds he made– it *was* pleasure-purring! She swallowed. He was opening his sensual senses to her.

His eyes were already dilating!

Soosha pressed her palms against the broad chest in an attempt to push him away from her.

It had no effect whatsoever.

The dance was over and he was going to take his prize. Rolling on top, Daxan captured her face between his hands and seized her mouth.

Claimed it.

His true feline persona was unmasked along with the untamed passion of her race. Of the males.

He *purred* down her throat as he staked his mating rights.

Her struggles were in earnest now.

It was a natural feminine reaction to a strong male predator. In the mating ritual, some Familiars stalked and hunted their unwary mates. The male usually triggered the response in the female, and some males liked to control that trigger. A Familiar would pursue his woman as if she was the only prey that counted. And he would adore doing it. It was called a T'kan. *A love hunt.*

As the saying goes, it was not for everyone.

Other races, such as the Spoltami, would never understand that aspect of Familiar mating.

Soosha did. But her understanding would not help her with Daxan. Her frantic exertions were nothing to his strength of will. Lips, velvety in texture, iron in determination, parted over her mouth.

Daxan was going to take what was his.

He captured her breath.

Inhaled completely to draw it down deep inside him. He seized everything.

The room began to spin and darken. Still Soosha tried to break away from his iron grip. Her balled fists pounded his chest.

In matters of mating, males were not inclined to be swayed. Daxan Sahain would not relent. She had come to take him and now *he* was taking her.

Soosha was on the very edge of losing consciousness.

Then he sent breath back to her! Just as ritual demanded. He blew into her mouth, filling her lungs with air, with renewed life.

His life.

And she greedily took it. She sucked in his gift of life.

From this point on, every breath she took would be his. In turn, with every breath she exhaled, she would give him renewal. In this way, they were mystically connected as one.

She was fastened to him forever.

Daxan had bound her to him for all eternity.

"Why did you not tell me?"

Soosha wasted no time confronting her new husband. She was hurt, confused, bewildered, and not a little apprehensive. He had deceived her. Could she ever trust him?

She would have to— he was her mate.

Daxan flung his glistening hair back over his shoulders. The more one stared at the gleaming mass, the more dazzling it became, Soosha realized. Since he was no longer hiding his true appearance from her, his beauty was spectacular.

What an exquisite Familiar male!

It amazed Soosha that he had been able to tone down such stunning features. She acknowledged that in his guise as a Spoltami, he had been exceedingly handsome. *But now ...!*

His expressive green and gold eyes were still hazy from

the exchange of breath they had just shared. "I hoped you would come to your senses and return to M'yan, Soosha. Word has been sent to me that your brother is on his way here this very moment. You would do well to realize how perfectly you have complicated the issue."

"Issue? What issue" She blinked, not sure what he was referring to. "You mean our mating?"

"That is exactly what I mean."

Soosha snarled, truly angry. "How dare you! You refer to your mating as an issue!"

Resting on his side of the bed, Daxan watched her, fascinated. A full-blown storm was developing right in front of him. The female cat came forth, hissing.

"I do not know which is worse! That you refer to our mating as an issue– or that you would send your mate away! What kind of a man are you?"

He clasped her shoulders. "The kind who would keep his wife alive!"

The loud crash of a door being kicked open– and the even louder roar of something *big* charging into the hallway below– made both Daxan and Soosha freeze.

Soosha clasped her handsome Familiar to her. She was still outraged at his deception, but he was, well, familiar.

"What is it?" she gasped in fright. "Do you think it is that awful man from the *sacri*?"

Daxan's brow furrowed. "I do not know; it sounds like a *xathu* beast has been set loose in my doorway."

In a single agile motion, he sprung off both her and the bed, unveiling the true, fluid movements of his race.

He grabbed a robe and his cuff, donning both as he strode to the door. More than anything else, Daxan's sleek, predatory stride revealed to Soosha exactly what he was–

No male moved like a Familiar male.

With every step, his lithe, sensual nature was revealed.

But who was he? And what was he doing on Spoltam? Soosha recognized that the situation was strange, to say the least.

For one, she had not been thinking of mating. If she had not come to Spoltam, her mating might not have occurred for months or even years.

Which brought up a second point. This man had also ignored the King's decree. He had either left M'yan after Gian Ren had the secret Tunnel sealed; or he had not obeyed the King's order to return home.

Either way, her husband was an outlaw.

Was he a rogue Familiar as well?

She bit her lip. He did not seem wild or uncontrollable– at least not any more wild or uncontrollable than most of their males.

What was more, he had not harmed her.

Just the opposite. He had protected her by bringing her into the safety of his home.

Of course, now she knew the true reason behind his actions. He had felt the Calling. Then he had sensed her. It probably was why he had come into the marketplace in the first place. To protect his mate.

As soon as he met her, he had actively triggered her.

Yet how had Daxan disguised himself? Soosha had never heard of a Familiar being able to do such a thing. Their unique dual-colored eyes always gave them away to others.

She was sure it had something to do with the cuff he wore on his forearm. *Where did he obtain it and just how much of an outlaw is he?*

Daxan had not wanted her to know he was Familiar until after the bond was sealed and they were mated.

That realization did not give her a comforting feeling.

Soosha put a hand to her throbbing forehead, rubbing the sore spot at the center. Such thoughts made one's head ache!

One thing was certain, as wild as Daxan had been the previous night– he was no where near as wild as he could have been. She knew that the surface of the man's stamina had not even been scratched.

So to speak.

He had held back in the very throes of the mating stance! Soosha did not want to even speculate at the capacity for sexual control such a man wielded.

Although she was sure he was going to enlighten her.

The terrified bleat of a Zot rent the air.

It was followed by the muffled thud of something heavy being hurled against an interior wall.

"Did you not know that Familiars dine on Zots? Now out of my way; I am coming in! I suggest that you get your master at once– for I am about to tear his abode apart and he might wish to witness the deed!"

Soosha's eyes widened. Brygar!

Her irascible brother was causing his usual mayhem! How had he found her so fast? The man could not track the path of a slime-oozing *zorph* through a dry sand bed!

Her thoughts were halted by another voice. One she was beginning to recognize with every pore of her body.

Except it sounded somewhat different. The smooth, mellow voice of Daxan Sahain was lowered to an ominous level– one he had never used with her. The commanding tone shocked her.

"No need to call me, I am here. Go back to the kitchens, *Zot*."

"B-b-but Master Sahain-"

"I said go back to the kitchens. I will handle this."

Soosha listened to see what would transpire next.

The meticulous *Zot* did not need to be told again.

He scurried through a door at the end of the hall, his tail swishing madly behind him.

Daxan leveled an icy look at his uninvited guest.

Said guest cared not a whit.

He squared his wide shoulders, threw back his head, and proclaimed in a proud voice, "I am Brygar from the Fifth Clan of the Familiar! You have my sister and I demand you release her at once!"

Daxan's amused snort could be heard all the way up the stairs.

It was certainly not the reaction Brygar expected.

"I know who you are, Brygar of the Fifth Clan."

"Well, I do not know *you*, Spoltami, and if you do not hand over my sister to me swiftly, it will soon be of no consequence who you *were*."

"Always charge in roaring, hmm, Brygar? You should

learn that clandestine entry serves better on occasion."

"I have tried to council him thus. It is, I vow, pointless."
A second man entered the house from the street. He had the
tall, authoritative mien of a Charl warrior.

Daxan arched his brow. What was this warrior-knight
doing with the Familiar Brygar? He had no wish to bring
the Charl into this! Especially a Charl who looked as
deadly as this green-eyed man. The Aviaran was not in
battle stance, yet, the sparks danced in his eyes.

He is powerful.

Despite the potential danger, strong mystical forces were
a pleasing balm to any Familiar. Pleasing and dangerous.
Familiar were always drawn to that combination.
Throughout time, the Familiar aligned themselves to the
wizards of Aviara for just that reason.

His power might explain why Brygar traveled with the
Charl, Daxan reasoned; but it did not explain the Charl's
presence.

"Brygar, your sister did not tell me she had a Charl
warrior, as well as a Familiar who thinks he has two sets
of *kani*, as her champions."

Traed corrected him immediately. "I am not a Charl."

Daxan was surprised. "You have the ability but not the
sanction?" He was not positive, but the man's power level
felt like it might be well past the fifth tier. Daxan had
never heard of an Aviaran of such power who was not of the
Charl. He was curious as to how such a situation was
allowed to stand. From what he knew, the High Guild was
very fussy about *those* kinds of things.

Traed ignored the man's question and in typical 'Traed'
fashion simply stared ahead, stone-faced.

"You see what I deal with?" Brygar, disgusted with

Traed's reserve, muttered to himself as he tried to peer into the shadows of the hallway to get a better view of their 'host'. "But you are half right, stranger; I do have two sets of *kani.*"

Traed quirked an eyebrow at Brygar.

He had learned over the past few days that the Familiar had a bating sense of humor. Brygar seemed to thrive on outrageous declarations.

Brygar glanced at Traed and said in mock seriousness, "Had you not heard, Charl-who-is-no-Charl? The extra set comes from Spoltami men who apparently have none. Their men lose them with their passionless logic." He turned back to Daxan. "Now *who* are you? Come out of the shadows that we might see who we are to kill!"

We? Traed gave Brygar another sidelong glance that held a wealth of meaning. Killing an unarmed man in his robe in his own home seemed a tad extreme to Traed.

Although, in certain circumstances, the idea could have appeal. . . . He glanced again at Brygar, only this time, his look was speculative. Perhaps if the man wearing the robe was also the man who boasted of two sets of kani?

Yes, that would be acceptable for him.

He shrugged off the fantasy. Reluctantly. "You have heard of attempting diplomacy first; have you not, Brygar?"

The Familiar grinned wickedly. "Truth be told, I care not for that method." He circled his arm through the air. Shinar y shinjii. "Thus it has no meaning for me."

"This does not surprise me." It was apparent that Brygar never willingly met a term he did not like. Clearly, this situation was going to get worse before it got better. Traed crossed his arms over his chest and leaned against the door frame.

Or what was left of the door frame after Brygar.

Sometimes there was naught to do but watch as foolishness unfolded. He sighed, then inquired of Daxan, "Have you had your midday meal yet?"

"My midday meal?" Daxan blinked. Were they both mad?

"You see, I feel better killing men before they have their midday meal. It seems uncharitable to end a man's life after he has dined. The meal makes the opponent sluggish. There is not as much fight in him."

Although the man spoke in a perfectly serious tone, the Aviaran's green eyes flashed ever so slightly in what could only be called dark humor.

"Thus if you have had your midday meal," the Aviaran went on, "I will probably wait until the morrow to slay you."

"Then I have definitely partaken of my midday meal." Daxan moved out of the shadowed alcove.

For once Brygar was speechless.

But it did not last long.

"*YOU!*"

Daxan's lips curled upward; he inclined his head in greeting. "I had no idea Familiar were so well-endowed, Brygar. My esteemed respects to your clan. Or . . . have you made off with all of their *kani* as well?"

"What are you doing here!" Brygar fumed and turned from Daxan to Traed. "What is he doing here?"

As if Traed should know.

Not moving from his post against the frame, Traed simply shrugged his shoulders. He had no clue and was not inclined to delve into it further.

141

Unless, of course, he had to.

Daxan motioned to Traed. "Come inside and close the door behind you before you alert the entire city of Aghni to your presence. "

Traed moved off the frame and attempted to close the door. After a few tries, the panel listed to the side but stayed in place.

"How did you two get here without being noticed?" Daxan narrowed his eyes. "Or did you?"

"Let me simply say that Brygar was moving very quickly. You may fill in that depiction on your own. I do not believe anyone took special note of him."

Daxan switched his attention fully to the tall Aviaran. "And you are?"

"Traed ta'al Krue." The Spoltami's amber eyes widened in recognition. He was familiar with some part of the name. It was not surprising to Traed. Krue was a well known Charl knight, and Traed, a legendary bladesman.

"Do not be so sure he was not spotted. The slavers are never seen, yet they are everywhere."

Traed nodded, thanking the stranger for the warning. By his sentiments, the man clearly was no threat to Brygar or his sister. It did not seem he wished them any harm. He addressed Brygar. "Do you mind telling me who our 'host' is since you seem to recognize him?"

"His name is Daxan Sa'ain and he is well-known to the family of Gian Ren. The man turned rogue and left M'yan– right after the Feast of Wizards, as I recall."

Traed listened carefully to Brygar's words. The Feast of Wizards was a Familiar celebration that honored the House of Sages. Every year, the entire High Guild of Aviara attended.

He turned and studied Daxan carefully.

Though few knew it– like his old master, Yaniff– Traed possessed the Sight. He focused on the ornate cuff around Daxan's forearm.

An Aviaran device of extraordinary skill.

The woven design was complex. Only a high level mystic would have the ability to conjure those kind of energy patterns. It was a rare, difficult bind to achieve, for it shielded truth. To do so, the spell had to continually warp the fundamental reality that surrounded the wearer.

The device would require regular 'feeding' by the wizard who created it.

Only a handful of wizards had the ability to conjure such a device.

Even less could sustain its continual drain.

Traed thought such devices were strictly controlled by the High Guild. In the wrong hands– or for the wrong purposes– stasis spells could prove disastrous.

So who had had given it to the Familiar?

He walked over to Daxan and lifted the man's forearm by the cuff. Arcs of twisting energy streamers flowed from Traed's hand to the armband, and Daxan's eyes revealed their true dual colors.

"Interesting." Traed murmured. "Might I ask who gave you this?"

Daxan met Traed's gaze but would not answer.

Traed was not surprised. He let go of the device. Once more the Familiar's green/amber eyes cloaked. "Should I bother to ask what are you doing on Spoltam or am I wasting my time on that as well?"

Daxan remained silent.

"I thought as much; however, I must insist that you–"

"He is an outlaw!" Brygar came forward. "There is no telling what mischief he is into! For all we know he could be working with Oberion slavers. *Where is Soosha?*"

"I am here, Brygar!" His sister's sweet voice floated down to the hall from above the stairwell. She peeked over the balcony at the men, her long black hair streaming over the railing like a gleaming ebony waterfall.

All three men paused in unison to enjoy the sight of such a beautiful girl.

Daxan almost purred as he remembered her silken hair twining around him. Its perfect scent. The sensuous ropes had held him to her exactly as he had imagined. He had been bound to her last eve in so many enticing ways.

He planned on getting most creative with that hair in the future. That was, if he lived to see M'yan again.

"Come down at once, Soosha! We need return home. We can discuss this foolish escapade of yours later."

Apparently, Brygar was not going to waste a moment getting her back to M'yan! Soosha felt like scratching him silly. *Foolish, thickskulled brother!*

"That is not possible, Brygar." Soosha sprinted the rest of the way down the stairs, her movements like a feather in the wind.

Brygar crossed his arms over his chest; he tapped his booted foot. "And why is it not possible?"

"Just a moment." Traed interrupted them both. "I need first hear more about why this man is wearing an Aviaran device—"

"Because we are *mated*, dear brother."

For Brygar, the news was too terrible to comprehend. "*What?!*" He roared, looking rapidly back and forth between the two of them.

144

There was no denying the satisfied aura surrounding that renegade, Daxan.

And, if he was truthful, his sister, as well.

Brygar chose to ignore that last part; much in the same way as he ignored the concept of diplomacy. If Soosha excelled at *shinar y shinjii*, then Brygar was its master. If something did not please him, he did his best to disregard it.

"*Not him*! Do not tell me it is so! Soosha, he has gone rogue! And besides, he has always made my mane stand on end. I do not like him!"

Soosha raised her chin and snarled back at her brother. "Then it is fortunate that *you* are not mated to him! You will accept him in our clan, dear brother, for he will be returning to live with us in our home!"

Daxan raised his brows, then rubbed his hand over his face as he listened to the siblings of squabble over him.

"You are an outlaw?" Traed asked hopefully.

"No."

The Aviaran's nostrils flared with annoyance and acute boredom.

But brother and sister were not paying them any mind; they were too busy having their own conversation.

Soosha scoffed at her brother's ridiculous reasoning. "It matters not if he is a rogue; he is still my mate!"

Daxan started to smile at her for standing by him– until she added, "The scoundrel will be returning to M'yan with us! You had best learn to call him brother."

Brygar was openmouthed with horror.

Traed thought the expression suited him. Furthermore, it rendered him *silent*.

Daxan, however, had something to say about it. "No, I

will not."

Neither brother or sister heard him.

Traed watched them all with a dangerous gleam in his eye. He could be at home at this moment, doing something useful. Like trimming the claws of his *phfiztger*. Surely that had more merit than this? How had he come to be here?

Ah, Yes. *Yaniff.*

"He cannot come!" Brygar threw his hands up in the air. "He is an outlaw!"

"That is not the reason." Daxan tried to interrupt but got nowhere.

"Pfft!" Soosha waved her hand in front of Brygar's nose. "Then Gian Ren will have to make him *not* be an outlaw!"

"Gian!" Brygar bellowed. "You will be lucky if the King does not expel you after what you have done!"

At this point Daxan motioned for Traed to take a seat. The battle showed no signs of abating.

The two of them sat down across from each other.

Traed calmly watched brother and sister snarl, roar, hiss, bellow, and screech at each other. "And to think I believed the House of Sages mad when they sent me with him," he murmured thoughtfully. "Now I am not so sure. He is a menace all by himself."

Daxan smiled. "I have heard of your 'relationship' with the High Guild. It must annoy you greatly to think they might be right– even one time."

Traed's head whipped back to Daxan. Like all Familiars, this one never let the opportunity to irk go by. Traed's jade eyes glittered.

Daxan chuckled.

"So, Daxan Sahain, you cultivate for *taj* Gian and who

else?"

The smile died on the Familiar's face. "You are very cunning for an Aviaran."

"Thus Yaniff sends me on these *important* journeys."

The man definitely had a subtle wit. Daxan lifted his hands palms up as if to indicate *'what can I say*?'

"As I see it, the King sent you to Spoltam to infiltrate these people and ascertain what, if any, threat level there is to M'yan."

"You begin to impress me, Charl."

"Therefore you left M'yan as a rogue Familiar to avoid suspicion."

Daxan winked.

"From what I have gathered you have been on Spoltam some time."

Daxan's reply was somewhat hesitant. "Yes."

Traed nodded. "Interesting."

Behind them an urn flew through the air, missing Brygar and sailing to within a hair's width of Traed's right ear.

Without missing a beat, he smoothly released his light blade and pulverized the pottery an instant before it would have shattered against the side of his head.

His weapon was retracted and back in his waistband before the first shards even hit the carpeted floor.

He calmly continued his conversation as if nothing untoward had occurred. "The armband you are wearing is quite complex. I have never seen one like it before. There are few who have the power to nurture such an intricate weave. Tell me who gave it to you."

Daxan sat back in his chair and steepled his fingers under his chin. "You know, you have the reflexes of a Familiar; it is quite extraordinary."

Traed was never a man to be sidetracked. Especially by an observation. He swung the lightblade around to Daxan's throat in a heartbeat. "With most weapons accuracy is more important."

Daxan did not even blink. "You would not want to do that, my friend," he said quietly.

"And why is that?"

"For one, I would kill you before your blade sliced into my skin."

Traed arched a brow. "So you all say. What is the other reason?"

"If you should manage to best me, you would then have to deal with *Soosha*." Daxan grinned broadly at the Aviaran.

His wise words gave Traed pause.

The female Familiar did not seem to listen to reason when it came to doing other than what *she* wanted. She was much like the brother. It would be foolish to provoke her. He glanced over his shoulder.

At that moment Soosha was holding her clawed hand in front of her brother's face, threatening to scratch him senseless. Traed arched his left eye-brow.

Daxan knew that the Aviaran could deal very well with Soosha– if he had to. But would he *want* to? That was another matter, entirely.

Despite the terrible threat of "Soosha unbound", the green-eyed man kept the blade securely at his throat. Daxan was impressed. "Of course there is my new brother Brygar and his two sets of kani to consider. . ."

Traed's eyelash flickered. Once.

Daxan snorted. He *is* finding this humorous. "At least he is not part of your family. Imagine my shock when I came down the stairs."

"I am not sure he is not part of my family– and that is what worries me," Traed quipped back.

Daxan threw back his head and roared with laughter.

Traed retracted his blade. But he remembered what Brygar had said: *"He went rogue just before the Feast of Wizards. . ."*

The connection did not seem coincidence and Traed needed to know the truth. It was his nature to always come back to that piece of the puzzle that would not fit. "Was Yaniff the one who gave the cuff to you?"

Daxan stared at him for long moments before speaking. "It is so important for you to know?"

"Yes."

"You believe it was Yaniff?"

"Yes."

"Does he concern you?"

Traed thought before he answered. "Concern is not the right word."

"Hmmm." Daxan crossed his ankle over his knee. "Gian has oft told me that most times it is better not to know the workings of mystics; for with such knowledge can come heartbreak and sorrow."

"I would rather sit with those companions than dine on deception."

"My senses tell me that you do sit with those companions, knight. Frequently."

Traed revealed nothing.

Daxan sighed. Charl were a breed apart. Even when they claimed not to be Charl. He would not get under this knight's skin; the man would never reveal anything he did not want revealed. "Very well, I will tell you this, but be forewarned. It may indeed sorrow your heart."

Traed steeled himself. "Go on."

Daxan fingered the intricate weavings in the cuff. "Look not to Yaniff in this."

Traed fully expected to hear the seventh-level mystic named as the conjurer. And now his heart was full of sorrow– just as the Familiar had predicted.

His suspicion had done Yaniff a disservice.

The old master meant more to him than he could ever say. When he was a child and ignored by the Guild and most of the Aviaran familial lines, Yaniff had taken him on as student. Later, he defied The House of Sages, claiming him as a son.

Charl ways ran deep. To this day he had never been able to truly refuse any request the old mystic made of him. The crafty wizard always managed to ensnare him in his schemes.

Yet. . . if it was not Yaniff, than who was it?

There were only a handful in the High Guild with that kind of power. The creation of such a device would have taken months and would have severely depleted the conjurer during its creation. Not to mention the continual drain of its maintenance.

Mayhap Yaniff did not create the cuff, a voice whispered to him. *Mayhap Yaniff instructed someone to make it. . .*

Questions. Always more questions!

Traed was not sure why the answers were so important; he just knew that they were.

Daxan carefully watched the play of thoughts cross Traed's features. Only a Familiar would have been able to discern the slightest change of mood; this Aviaran was a master at keeping his emotions hidden.

There was more here than Daxan cared to explore–but, then, he was not Charl. He had enough on his own to deal with. He attempted to lighten the topic. "Of course, to make the chronicle clear, Traed ta'al Krue, Familiar do not actually have two sets of–"

Traed put his hand up. "That is more knowledge than I require."

The room behind them suddenly became still.

Traed turned around in his seat– just to see if the two had finally killed each other off and he could go home.

He viewed the scene before him in amazement. Brother and sister were hugging each other *and* smiling.

Apparently after the snarling and hissing were done, all was then forgotten. The two of them were beaming like a happy pair of tuned crystals.

Traed sighed stoically.

Brygar, grinning a cheery, white-toothed smile, announced to the room at large: "My sister and I are in agreement! The rogue who has no pride will come home with us!"

Daxan immediately stood. "No. I am not going back to M'yan."

Soosha ran over to him, the smile dying on her face. "But Daxan, you must. . ." She trailed off, not quite sure what to say to convince this man who knew her in body but had yet to learn her fully in mind.

"*Soosha*." Daxan cupped her cheek with his palm. "I am here at Gian Ren's behest. I cannot leave."

"You-you mean you are not an outlaw after all?"

He shook his head, then dipped down to let his lips lightly caress hers. "No," he breathed. "I am trying to help our people. The Tunnel between Spoltam and Ganakari breeds danger for us. Should Spoltam join forces with their *Tunnel-match*, Ganakari, our people will be in even more danger and so will the Alliance. I must remain on Spoltam, Soosha."

Soosha bit her lip and cast her eyes down. "For how long, husband?"

His hands clasped hers, bringing them to his lips. Already he was in love with her. Already he felt the pain of their parting.

He would die a little each day without her beside him.

But his people needed him and they all would have to sacrifice to survive. "Until such time that Spoltam either enters the Alliance or turns against us. There is no other way. I am the eyes and ears of the royal house."

"Then I will stay with you, Daxan Sa'ain."

Her offer came as a shock to him. He knew she was not overly fond of this world– and with good reason. She had almost been hunted down and enslaved moments after her arrival.

Right then, he saw the qualities in her that he had always yearned for in a mate. In truth, he had been wild for her from the moment he had first spotted her leaping from stall to stall in the marketplace, causing pandemonium wherever she went.

Laughing all the while.

Her laugh would carry him to any sacrifice. Because the sound of that laughter, so pure, so free, so joyous, represented everything a Familiar should fight to preserve.

He had been forced to contain his heart. His wife did not know him yet as he truly was– she did not know that he would lick the tip of her ear just to see her smile.

Or that he cried in secret when his thoughts strayed to his lost family.

But there would come a time when they would all be free again and his children would play under the light of many different suns.

{*Are you sure about this, Soosha?*} He sent his thought privately to her.

{*Yes. I will stay with you, Daxan.*}

{*It will be dangerous.*}

{*I am a Familiar; I thrive on danger.*}

He looked at her with pride. {*You will have to stay hidden. My armband will not work on you.*}

{*No trips to the sacri?*}

His cheeks curved. {*No. Especially not the sacri.*}

{*Not even once?*} She asked, beguiling him in the way of her kind.

{*Not even once. Think you I would lose you to the slavers?*} His tongue slipped teasingly between her fingers.

{*You can always say I am your Familiar love slave.*}

He paused to stare up at her over their joined hands. {*They would be more apt to believe the reverse is true.*}

Soosha sucked in her breath at his revealing expression. The honed, intelligent features enthralled her. This man who was her mate was an enigma. Cunning, yet methodical. Sensual, yet controlled. In the darkest hours of night, he was as untamed as any Familiar. . . yet he was an incredibly sensitive lover.

There were things that Daxan did to her, things that she had never. . .

Her heart pounded as she looked into his eyes. She knew in that moment that they would find so much passion, so much love together. They were complete opposites but they were exactly matched.

He was her adventure!

Without hesitation she turned to her brother. "I have decided to remain here on Spoltam with my husband."

Brygar stared at his sister, dumbfounded.

Traed silently counted the moments for the statement to hit the big Familiar's brain. *One. Two. Thr-*

"You cannot remain here! It is too dangerous. I will not allow it!"

Since Brygar's stubbornness seemed in no danger of taking a journey on the path to enlightenment, Traed picked up a thick tome lying on the table by his chair. It mattered not that he did not read Spoltami.

At the rate Brygar processed acceptance, Traed acknowledged he should become a scholar in the language.

He propped his legs on the opposite chair and crossed his booted feet.

Daxan was not as patient as the Aviaran. He stepped forward to face the dark-haired Familiar, nose-to-nose.

"It may interest you to know that I agree with you; Spoltam is dangerous for her. I believe she should return to M'yan. Nevertheless, Soosha has made her decision and I must respect it. Your sister will remain on Spoltam with me. Best you accept it now to avoid problems later. And know this as well, Brygar. . . I will never take orders from *you*."

Not the most soothing declaration to state to *this* particular Familiar, Traed concluded. He opened the first page of the book.

As expected, Brygar's brow lowered ominously. "*Really*. And whose house will you enter when you return to M'yan? Hmmm? You have none of your own, as I recall. It is *my* clan that will bring you in, if we—that means *I*— so choose."

A muscle in Daxan's jaw ticked. It was true; he had no close family remaining. They had been among the first of the Familiars to disappear. Perhaps, like him, they had always chosen the most dangerous, most remote places to explore?

He had vowed to revenge their loss, which was one reason he was Gian's eyes and ears in the most dangerous of missions.

Still, a Familiar with no clan was little more than a renegade. Such Familiars were called Loners and they were considered dangerous, for they often had allegiance only to themselves.

Brygar's words hurt Daxan more than the brash Familiar knew or probably ever intended.

"Then I will start my own house. There is still some of the clan left. . ."

Brygar found out what he had been seeking. Daxan had some spit. And that pleased him. "You will do no such thing. You will come to my house where you *will* belong and you will like it!"

Daxan's stance relaxed. "Very well then."

Brawl averted. Traed reclined in his chair, booted feet extended, arms crossed over his chest. He closed his eyes. The journey with Brygar had been a ceaseless sprint in every which direction. Traed refused to remember what they had gone through to get free of the mud bog on Mollock; the Familiar's lack of directional sense seemed to be compensated with a never-ending supply of vigor.

"Your sister will be helping your people, Brygar. Under those circumstances, *taj* Gian will most likely overlook her transgressions. " Traed laced his fingers behind his neck and stretched out. "Her flight from M'yan might have been inevitable. She was destined to mate Daxan. Even a king cannot stand between that."

Brygar thumped his own forehead. "By Aiyah, the Charl-who-is-not-Charl is correct! How, oh, how, could I have not seen this?" He snorted derisively.

Traed opened one eye. "Never ask for my advice again, Familiar."

"I do not recall asking for it this time."

"Due to your witless nature, I have been allowing you free reign with a certain level of irritation. You are close to using up your allotment." Traed closed his eyes again.

Brygar nudged his sister. "Look, Soosha, he meditates like a Charl."

Still relaxed, Traed's hand went to his waistband. His fingers slowly tapped the hilt of his lightsaber in warning.

Soosha slapped her brother on the arm for goading the solemn Aviaran. The man's jade eyes sparked with strong power. If he did not wish to be called Charl, then so be it. There was no telling what he was capable of doing should her brother annoy him one time too many.

Soosha worried her lip. The handsome knight was a bit forbidding; albeit somewhat fascinating. His power level was one of the strongest she had ever felt.

She had heard tales of Charl lovers– of how they sparked when they made love and their desire ran hot. She observed the seemingly relaxed stance of this knight. His posture did not fool her. If attacked, he would have his blade slicing the air in an instant.

As a woman, she could not help but wonder what this cool Aviaran would be like when he disrobed in the dark and his awesome power truly unlocked. What unruly passions would he unleash?

By the look of him, more than most would be able to handle.

Brygar proclaimed that he would remain with Soosha long enough to assure himself that his sister was being accorded all of the comforts that *he* deemed worthy of her.

In other words, he would insure that the "Spoltami" treated Soosha to any and every luxury she desired.

Which meant whatever *he* desired.

To say that Daxan Sa'ain's mettle was put to the test was an understatement.

Brygar's constant demands drove the golden-haired Familiar to the brink of madness.

Traed could not understand Brygar's view of the situation. Brygar continued to refer to Daxan as the "Spoltami" (to Daxan's face, no less, which irritated the man no end). Traed suspected that Brygar would forever refer to Daxan thus.

Never mind that the man was Familiar.

To Brygar, it mattered not. Shinar y shinjii.

"Your brother drives me mad."

Daxan's lips feathered the side of Soosha's throat.

"Must we talk of him now?" Soosha winked at her stunning husband as she rubbed her hipbones against the ripple of muscle on his abdomen. His skin was velvety smooth; the muscles beneath, solid.

Once again, his glorious mane was confined in twisted coils. The beaded ends wandered over her collarbone, leaving scores of tingling caresses in their wake.

As much as Soosha loved his hair unbound, there was something to be said for these coils too. Last eve, he had shown her some of interesting uses for them she would not have thought possible.

The heat rose inside her just thinking about it.

Daxan had started to introduce to his true brand of pleasure. Sensually, he was devastating. There was a commanding, intense quality to him that turned incendiary when he was with her.

From her own experience, she knew that every Familiar had a unique expertise with lovemaking. The resultant experience was always memorable.

But Daxan. . . ! Well, *he* was tuned just to her. She *loved* the way he stroked her!

"When are we to discuss him, then?" Daxan rubbed his chin across the top of her head. "He keeps me in his sights every minute of the day! Do not let his relaxed bearing fool you, Soosha. Should I happen to stroll out onto one of the balconies– there he is! Lounging on chair as if he had always been there!"

Soosha put her hand over her mouth and giggled.

"Laugh not. When I go into the kitchens, he is leaning against a wall, pretending to watch the kitchen *Zot*

159

prepare the meal."

Soosha rolled her eyes. "Surely you are imagining this, Daxan?"

"Am I? This morning when I left our chamber to go downstairs, he was in the hallway."

"So? Perhaps he was leaving his chamber as well?"

"He was lounging across the portal of our door."

Soosha scratched her chin. "Was it a sunny place? He likes to do that in the—"

"*Soosha.*"

"There is naught I can do, Daxan! He is the leader of our clan and. . ."

Daxan's nostrils flared. His head bent until their noses touched. "And what?"

"He is my brother." She shrugged.

"Mmmm." Daxan rubbed his nose along the tip of hers. "Would you not at least allow me to knock him over the head? Just for a few days. . . I promise he will enjoy the rest."

Soosha smiled as his rigid member pressed between her thighs. Her husband was annoyed— but not distracted from his main goal. A true Familiar.

"You will come to love him; you will see."

"Of *that* I need to be convinced." His teeth captured her lower lip in a Familiar love bite known as the *kitten's kiss*. Then he quickly licked the tip of her ear. His lips twitched with amusement at the sound of her laughter.

Soosha's catlike expression danced with invitation. {*Oh, I am very good at convincing, husband.*}

Daxan growled, accepting her challenge. {*Let us see how good you truly are then.*}

Soosha was more than happy to show him.

It was not long before Daxan Sa'ain purred in complete agreement: she was most excellent at convincing.

Soon, he was even shouting his opinion. If not his agreement.

To the walls. To the ceiling. To the flooring.

And, oddly enough, to the center column in the room.

Traed was more than ready to return to Aviara.

Unfortunately, he had yet to convince that irritating dolt to depart!

It seemed that once the huge Familiar 'took' to a place, he settled himself in and would not be budged!

Finally– after they had been on Spoltam for several days– Soosha slapped her 'paw' down.

"Brother, I think it best you return to M'yan."

Brygar did not even glance up from the gooey delicacy he was eating. "Mmmm. And why is that, Soosha?"

"My husband claims that he will be forced to kill you if you remain one more day."

Brygar paused briefly before taking another bite of the Spoltami confection. "Does he?" He licked the edge of his finger. Slowly. Deliberately.

"*Yes, I do.*" Daxan padded into the room.

Traed noted that their host's eyes were narrowed to slits

of boiling anger. If the man had been Aviaran, he surely would have been sparking.

Which meant this might become interesting.

By Aiyah, Traed rued, *if only I could place a wager. . .* !

"The time has come for you to leave, Brygar."

"For what reason do you so speak?"

Brygar seemed to view the world with a dense lens. Traed raised his eyebrows and then sat back to watch the entertaining situation unfold.

"For one, you are putting my house in danger each day you remain."

"Hmm..." Unconcerned, Brygar took another chomp of the sticky sweet. "And the other reason?"

"I have acceded to your every demand, your every whim, for days. You are running my household into exhaustion! What is more, you watch me day and night. *I cannot take a breath without you.* I have had enough of it!"

"Ahhhh!" Brygar put the confection down. "Finally the cat shows *claw*. If this so bothers you, why have you allowed it?

"Because you are Soosha's brother! I wish to please her. But I find I can no longer allow this to go on!"

Brygar nodded slowly. "Good. THAT is what I was waiting for." He stood to his full height, towering over everyone in the room.

Soosha gasped.

Daxan faced Brygar, every muscle bunched to spring.

Traed watched and waited; his hand close to his lightblade. Yaniff would not look kindly upon him if these two tore each other to pieces. A great pity, to be certain.

Surprising everyone, Brygar suddenly threw back his head and roared with laughter. "You care enough for her that you have allowed me to command your house; and still you are man enough to slit my throat!"

He spread his large, muscular arms wide and clapped Daxan inside a strangle hold. Almost lifting the other Familiar off his feet. "A good balance!"

Daxan was too stunned to move.

Not that he could if he wanted to.

"Ha!" Brygar turned to Soosha. "You see? He treasures me like a brother already!"

"Let go of me, you fool!"

Soosha's eyes filled with tears of happiness. "Oh, Brygar, how could he not love you?"

That was when Traed ta'al Krue decided that one could never fully understand the feline race.

One could only deal with them.

And so, all was well.

Until, that is, they left for the Tunnels.

Daxan had recommended they use a more obscure Tunnel point than the one they had arrived in.

For safety sake, he urged them to use one of the Tunnels in a village a day's journey from Aghni. The small village was used by many trading caravans as it avoided the congestion of Aghni. In addition, the small village was a triconduit, connected to three different Tunnels– all unmonitored by the Charl.

Daxan had given explicit instructions.

The first Tunnel connected to a way point which led directly to Aviara.

The second Tunnel led to Ganakari. To be avoided at all costs.

The third, to an even more dangerous place, best left unexplored.

Traed and Brygar found the village easy enough and the journey along the seashore had been almost pleasant. Indeed,Traed had only been forced to threaten Brygar with mortal injury but a handful of times.

That ended when they reached the bluff that signified the Tunnelpoints.

Brygar counted the Tunnel entrances from left to right instead of right to left, as Daxan had instructed.

Of course, the brash Familiar immediately pivoted to vault into the wrong Tunnel.

Traed could not believe it. *He would not do this again! He would not.*

"Halt, Brygar! That is not the right–"

Too late.

It took Traed several moments– as he stood rooted in front of the pulsating maw– to duly comprehend that his erstwhile traveling companion had blithely entered a doorway to a world they had been warned was 'best left unexplored'.

He pinched the bridge of his nose and shook his head from side to side.

Well, there was no hope for it.

If he did not bring the Familiar back, Yaniff would never let him hear the end of it.

And he supposed Gian Ren might have something to say as well.

Why is it that every family has one Brygar?

Nothing was as dangerous as entering an unmonitored Tunnelpoint! He ground his teeth. *Ah, the joy of the quest.*

There was no telling what would greet him on the other

side.

Drawing his light saber from his waistband, he carefully stepped into the Tunnel.

What greeted him was a swift, strong blow to the head.

He was immediately knocked unconscious.

Traed came awake to the annoying sight of Brygar.

"I will kill you, Familiar." He rasped, then groaned as his own voice set off waves of pain in his head. "As soon as I can stand, you are finished."

Since Traed had been threatening to kill him on a regular basis since they had set out, Brygar was not too concerned. Except. . . the Aviaran rather looked as though he *meant* it this time.

"You will need to stand in line, Charl warrior." Brygar nodded to the other beings surrounding him.

As he became fully alert, Traed realized that the Familiar was chained to a rough post in the ground. Six Oberion slavers stood guard over him.

Traed stood up slowly, unsteady on his feet. His head was pounding from the viscous blow. He assumed his ears were ringing as well– until he realized he was dragging his own chains with him.

His shirt, his lightsaber, and his cape were gone; presumably stolen along with the leather thong that tied back his hair. He was surprised they had left him his *tracas* and boots.

There were dampening fields around Tunnel points; he probably would not be able to use any of his power to get them back. *A perfect ending to this foolish journey!*

Several hanks of hair fell into his eyes, annoying him. It mirrored the situation on Mollock– only without the constant deluge and scintillating scenery.

He tried to toss the hair out of his face; his mind endeavoring to comprehend the absurdity of what had occurred. Mayhap if he told Brygar to leap into danger, the dolt would hesitate? *By the blood of Aiyah*, did he never think to look before he reacted?

{*IT SEEMS WE HAVE WALKED INTO A TRAP, CHARL-WHO-IS-NO-CHARL!*}

Traed actually grimaced in pain. Now, on top of everything else, the *bellow-breath* was in his head!

And he could not even send his thoughts without roaring! Traed's injured skull pounded unmercifully.

He grabbed the sides of his head in agony. "Cease this clamor at once!"

{*It seems we have walked into a trap, Charl-who-is-no-Charl.*}

The man was a dimwit.

"Again I hear 'we'." He deadpanned back to the Familiar.

One of the slavers gave Traed a curious look, wondering what he was talking about. "Who do you speak to?"

Traed looked at the slaver and slowly widened his eyes. As if the blow to his head had jiggled his brains. "Do you not see it?"

168

"*Nagor Bati-s-s-s!*" The slaver spit on the ground and quickly looked away. Like the desert nomads of Zarrain, Oberions were notoriously superstitious. Madness made them uneasy.

Considering this was Traed, one of the most staid, logical, rational warriors-knights on Aviara, the concept was rather humorous to Brygar. The Familiar roared with laughter.

His chains were immediately, painfully tightened by the guards.

His laughter quickly turned into a snarl.

"So, you are a Charl warrior. . ." One of the others spoke. He was completely enshrouded in clothing; Traed could not see his face clearly. "I thought as much and so took the necessary precautions to subdue you."

Traed glanced at Brygar; he had purposely given them the impression that he was a Charl warrior. The Familiar might have no sense of direction but– as Traed was beginning to learn– Brygar was crafty.

And more astute than he ever let on.

The leader scurried over to Traed. "I want no trouble with you, Charl. The guards begin to realize they have attacked a warrior-knight. *Bad reflux.* We do not seek that kind of fortune."

Traed went silent. Like all excellent warriors, he had the patience to listen first. Early on, Yaniff had trained him thus: "*. . . listen down to the the grains of sand, Traed, then sift the granules through your mind to see what stays behind. . .*"

So he waited and filtered. And learned more than he would have thought possible.

"We have paid a Spoltam beggar to come through the

Tunnel to release you once we are gone." The Oberion grinned, showing a black maw of rotted teeth. "To show our good will to the Alliance."

Traed gave the leader a piercing look. "Mayhap, you should show your good will by releasing both of us now."

"I am afraid that is not possible. You see, we have plans for your robust, handsome friend. By the markings on his inner thigh, he is in his prime. He has a long life ahead of him. A long life of *service* to the Oberion empire."

Traed ignored the leader and turned to Brygar. "You allowed them to look at your inner thigh?"

Brygar shrugged. "It is obvious their males need something to aspire to."

The chains were yanked tighter. Brygar hissed. Like all Familiar, he hated the tether more than the pain.

He was soon to hate other things.

One of the guards grabbed Brygar by the hair, yanking his head back. He tried to force a thick fluid down the Familiar's throat. Brygar struggled in earnest now.

The huge Familiar almost succeeded in knocking over all six of the guards.

But the Oberion elixir need not be swallowed to be effective. A few droplets seeped into his skin. It was enough to weaken him.

Eventually they were able to wrestle him down and pour the rest of the drug down his throat.

The sight of it infuriated Traed, who had always detested injustice of any kind. He closed his eyes and tried to draw the power to him, but it was useless. The dampening fields were too strong.

Brygar tried to focus on Traed as his eyes clouded over from the drug. "Do not come looking for me, Charl!"

170

Traed paused and quirked his brow. "You still think to tell me what to do, Familiar?"

Brygar delivered a challenging grin. {*Ah, but I just did.*}

Mayhap Brygar really did have two sets of *kani*.

Traed smiled slightly as he realized that the drug they used was not the drug that had been given to Gian Ren. That one blocked a Familiar's special senses entirely.

Brygar was still able to send his thoughts. *And he was letting Traed know.*

What was more, considering the amount they had given him, the huge Familiar was not as drugged as he should have been.

Brygar would be no easy adversary for these slavers.

There would come a time when he would stubbornly fight. Probably to the death.

Traed called out to him. "Try not to get yourself killed until I have found you."

{*I had no idea you cared, Charl-who-is-no-Charl.*}

Traed shrugged, "It is a simple matter. If you are to be killed, then I reserve the pleasure."

Brygar let out a bark of laughter then became more serious than Traed had ever seen him.

His lavender and aqua eyes met Traed's squarely. Sincerely. {*Do not take too long, friend.*}

Traed nodded curtly. "You have my word on it."

Assured, Brygar grinned tauntingly up at his captors as he was dragged off. "What say you we play a game of *catch-and-kill* before the journey starts?"

The slaver on his right clubbed him on the head, knocking him out.

Traed grimaced. Best he find the brash Familiar quickly before the man irritated his captors into slaughtering him.

The Oberion leader spoke. "Consider him dead to all who knew him, Charl, for once we Oberions take him into our worlds, he will be lost forever. He will disappear. If you have a notion of liberating him, you would do well to forget it. He is our *property* from this day forward. We do not relinquish what we own."

Traed was not concerned with the Oberion's advice. "Actually, I am trying to decide which will come first. . ."

" And what is that?"

"Finding him or finding *you*."

Traed had a great effect on the Oberion, for he shook with fear. "You would do better to remember that Charl are not openly welcomed in the Oberion Empire. We have no wish to upset such a renowned group, of course; yet, you must ask yourself what example a Charl might set, coming into our worlds, uninvited, to force his ways upon us."

"I will take my chances." Traed promised in a low murmur, close to the slaver's face.

The Oberion paled. "Th-there are those planets, non-Alliance members, who would not look kindly upon such actions. They may think twice about joining your Alliance. There could be repercussions. Sides could be chosen. . . . Who can say what would happen?"

Certainly not Traed. He stared mutely at the Oberion leader.

"And all over one loud-speaking Familiar. You may look upon this advice as a favor, knight. We Oberions look out for our friends the Charl by sparing them this potential, disastrous embarrassment."

In a flash, Traed became keenly focused on the Oberion's chatter, but not for the alarm it held–

It was Yaniff's forewarning that overlapped the

Oberion's prattle.

Just a wizard's words–

Ever simple. Ever insightful.

"Go after him now," his old master had said. *"Before he causes a galaxian war. . ."*

As promised, a Spoltami beggar arrived to release Traed shortly after the slavers left, dragging an unconscious Brygar with them.

Traed made his way back to Aviara, his mind heavy with the events that had transpired.

It was no surprise that Soosha had not returned with him.

By his silence, Yaniff had hinted such might be the case.

Traed was becoming an expert on understanding Yaniff. The true reason he had been sent on this journey was very clear as well. It had never been for Soosha.

It had always been for Brygar.

"Go after him now," his old master had said. *"Before he causes a galaxian war. . . "*

Yaniff had covertly charged him as Chin t'se leau to the huge Familiar. By Aviaran law, Traed was now bound to be the Familiar's watchman.

Once again, the old Sage had ensnared him in his magician's game and he was caught by his honor.

The wizard had delivered him by his own promise!

He was honor bound now to find and rescue Brygar, the Familiar. From what Yaniff hinted, there was much at stake.

But where did he start?

Before the Oberions left, Traed overheard the leader instruct one of his group, '. . . *Sell this one to Muklak Kargigion's tribe. That Oberion will know how to handle him. Kargigion will break him just enough to get top price for him.'*

But Traed knew that Brygar was not a man to be easily broken. Not that Familiar. He would never give in.

And so, the leader of the Fifth Clan of Familiar undoubtedly would be put to the lash and worse.

Still, there was one thing the Oberion slaver did not count on when he had left Traed, still shackled, to await the Spoltam beggar. While he might have been bound physically; he could still roam.

The Sight was not always dampened by the fields around Tunnels.

In this instance, he had been able to "see" the group up until the time they entered the next Tunnel point.

So Traed had a starting point for his search and woe to Muklak Kargigion when he found him!

But first, he need return to Aviara to apprise the House of Sages of the situation. He would confront Yaniff; after which, he would go for Brygar.

For that was the way the tale was to be written.

By Aiyah.

Yaniff set a warm cup of mir on the table in front of Traed.

"It is a pitiful thing, a Familiar with no sense of direction." He sat across from the tall Aviaran.

"You might have mentioned that to me *before* I left on your venture." Traed lifted the cup to his lips and sipped the fragrant brew.

Yaniff's eyes, darker than the darkest night, twinkled with mirth. "And be accused of boring you?"

Traed gave the mystic his customary stony response.

Yet Yaniff's words rang in his head. It was a sad fact that people were often praised and condemned for their differences.

Often the *same* differences at that.

After due contemplation, he arched his brow. *Can truth, itself, be an unfolding paradox?*

"You are an intriguing student, Traed."

"I am not your student."

"Ah." Yaniff glanced up to the rafters at Bojo's sudden squawk. "Yes, you are right; that is for another day." He poured them both a second cup of *mir.* "I take it Brygar has followed his usual path and now finds himself in danger?"

Traed nodded. "Grave danger."

The old sage clucked his tongue. "Truly a predicament." He sipped his drink and waited for Traed to speak.

"You expect me to find him, do you not?"

Yaniff shrugged. "Whatever you wish, *student-who-is-no-student.*"

Traed's jaw ticked. "Do not play your games with me. The man has been captured by slavers! He will suffer greatly. You would never leave such an abomination *alone.*"

Yaniff took another slow sip of his drink. "It has naught to do with me. I do not owe the man anything. . ." He glanced slyly up at Traed. "*Do you?*"

Yes, he did.

He had promised Brygar he would rescue him. He was the Familiar's sworn protector!

As well Yaniff knew.

What was more, with this oath, he had taken on the mien of a Charl knight. Throughout time, Charl and Familiar shared a special bond. Wizards protected their Familiars and Familiars were their instruments.

But the bond went deeper.

The tie between them was mystical in nature, for both were enjoined by the power wielded so expertly by the Charl knights.

Yaniff stared at Traed knowingly.

Traed placed his palms flat on the table and leaned forward. "Do not gaze upon me like that."

"Like what?" Yaniff set his drink down and picked up a

an ancient book of spells that was lying on the table. He began to peruse the Grimmoire, absentmindedly.

"Will you answer my next question?"

"Yes."

"Could you have prevented this?"

The lines on Yaniff's face deepened. "No."

Traed's chair scrapped the wooden floor as he rose. "Why do I let this happen?"

There is nothing quite like the chafing sting of an old wizard's chuckle.

Traed's nostrils flared with annoyance. "Tell the Guild I go not for them. I go because I am bound by my oath."

"We both know it is because you have no heart, Traed."

The solemn Aviaran's cheekbones darkened to bronze. "Enough! Leave me be, wizard!" He stormed out of the cottage, slamming the door behind him.

Yaniff lifted his arm and Bojo flew from the rafters to perch on his shoulder. The old wizard softly stroked the downy feathers of his beloved winged companion.

"Never, Traed," he whispered aloud as Bojo cooed in ecstasy. "*Never.*"

Daxan led Soosha to one of their favorite spots on top of the cliff behind their home.

When they reached the summit, he rested against the rock wall, drawing her back against him. Much as they had done from the first.

His strong arms encircled her waist as both watched the play of moonlight flickering across the Spoltam sea.

This was their favorite time of day. Night.

They could be themselves on this cliff, away from the watchful eyes of Aghni natives. Daxan's chin nudged along Soosha's shoulder in a tender caress.

With every moment that passed, with each word he spoke, with every kiss, every touch– Soosha loved him more and more.

Oh, how she loved him!

He was like the glittering sea before them. Exotically beautiful on the surface, intricate and fathomless beneath.

With each encounter, Daxan revealed more of himself to her. Although he had never done so in the past, he was not afraid to share himself fully. Deeply.

He gave her everything.

She responded with no less.

Soosha thought back to the day when she had made her choice to defy a king and seek adventure.

She had found her adventure.

The days on Spoltam were not easy. She had to remain confined within the walls of the estate, most often covered. Even though Daxan trusted his servants, Soosha had to remember to always cast her eyes down when speaking to them.

Still, she would make the same choice today. Daxan was helping their people to survive and she was there equally by his side.

To be truthful, it was not all bad.

There were the wondrous sunsets of Spoltam; as well a constant supply of *Nightfall* to enjoy.

There were evenings like this one, where the beauty of the sky, the stars, and the sea forever etched into her senses; like the warm, arms holding safe.

Holding her with love.

And there was Daxan; her one, true match.

Yes, she had made the best choice.

Because when she was with him, everything was right.

Yaniff made his way through the woods to the House of Sages.

It was a pleasant journey.

A slight breeze was in the air, the sun was shining, and the joyful songs of sylvan creatures filled the forrest.

With each jaunty step, he swung a distinctive token back and forth.

Arriving at the House of Sages, he sought out one of its members. He found his mark dozing by a fountain in the inner court.

Gently, he shook the old man awake.

"Urrrmm?" The wizard Ernak rubbed his eyelids. "Is it time for the evening meal, then?"

Yaniff smiled softly. "Not yet, old friend. I woke you because I have a gift for you."

The kindly mystic's eyes popped wide with delight; he was clearly charmed by the surprise. *"For me?"*

Another wizard might have been more inquisitive about such a gift. Ernak was not a complex thinker; and, thus, had never mastered the art of exquisite wizardry.

He had, however, mastered the art of happiness.

No small feat, Yaniff acknowledged to himself. On some days, Ernak was truly an inspiration. *Is it his simplicity that allows him to find happiness?* Or is he just a simple man?

No matter.

Rare was the wizard, indeed, who had peace of mind and a light heart.

Ernak examined his gift, gasping with joy. "A *Zot* basket! Why, I have always wanted one of these! They are very difficult to come by, you know; *Zots* hate to part with them. To what do I owe this wondrous pleasure, Yaniff?"

Yaniff clapped him on the back. "There are often days that trouble me, Ernak; yet, when I look at you, so at peace, it gives me hope that the perspective of the world can always change. It simply depends on the view. Thus, I wanted to thank you for being you, my friend. Just for being you."

Ernak gave him an endearing, bashful smile, clearly stunned by this unwarranted praise from the most revered mystic on Aviara. "I do not know what to say. . . "

""Pfft!" Yaniff waved his gratitude away. "The wise man knows when to be silent."

Ernak chuckled. "I confess I am often at a lack for words so I must be very wise indeed."

Yaniff glanced covertly around the courtyard, then lowered his tone to a conspiratorial whisper. "I will share a secret with you, Ernak."

"What is it?" Ernak whispered back, leaning in towards

Yaniff with eyes expectantly wide.

"Sometimes it is better to remain silent than to say anything at all. You would be surprised how many are willing to interpret silence as weighty thinking."

"Really?"

"Yes, so you see there is no need to thank me. I will simply interpret your loss of words as the ponderous silence of gratitude befitting a wise Sage!" Yaniff grinned slyly at him.

Ernak stroked his chin. "I never thought of silence in such a way before. . ."

"Fascinating, is it not?"

"Hmmm. . . yes. Yes, it is. . ."

"Perhaps when next the High Guild sits in chamber, you will see for yourself its remarkable power?"

Ernak took to the suggestion at once. He nodded enthusiastically. "Mayhap I will!"

Yaniff clapped him on the back as they left the courtyard together.

And so, when next the House of Sages convened, a mysterious stalemate occurred. . .

With six Sages against and six Sages approving, the deciding vote remained steadfastly silent.

Throughout the meeting, it was remarked that the gentle wizard Ernak was strangely aloof.

Affecting the pose of the deep thinker, his eyes stared fixedly at the far stone wall. It was as if he contemplated the very grains of mortar that held, not simply the wall, but the entire universe in place!

He would not speak.

Frustrating both sides.

Half of the wizards argued that the fate of the universe was at stake by not voting! The other half maintained that the continuum had nothing what-so-ever to do with the vote!

Regardless, the vote had to be postponed, so no action was taken. Thirteen ballets must be cast for a decision to be valid. It was Aviaran law.

Ernak's unprecedented silence baffled his peers.

All, that is, save one.

If a few Sages questioned the satisfied sparkle in that wizard's eye, none dared voice it. Moreover, if the subject of the proposed ruling just happened to be a student of that mystic—

It might be coincidence.

Wizards were a very pragmatic lot. Especially old wizards.

And while there had been no decision; the day had not been completely wasted.

No, never wasted.

For there is always contemplation of the evening meal to soften the pitiless rigors of a mystic's life.

And to those who wonder if wizards waste time pondering such trivialities—

They pass along this assurance:

"Assortment is, after all, our business."

Epilogue

The Silver Forest, Planet Ganakari

Deep in the Sylvan Woods, where trees are dense and leaves form a thick sheltering blanket, stands a simple cottage.

Inside the hut, a rickety bed has been moved as close to the flames of a midday fire as safety will allow. On that bed lies a huddled, nameless mass of *something* barely alive.

The day is not a cold one, yet even under the piles of ragged blankets that have been heaped upon the bed, what lies beneath shivers uncontrollably.

So far, nothing has risen from the ashes of the flames; whatever lies here sinks further into the cold desolation of its own destruction.

Outside, an old woman slowly gathers sticks of firewood from the forrest floor. She pauses a moment to lean against a tree.

This woman has a great gift of healing; however, this task might be beyond her talents. Each day that passes, wounds stitch, but darkness grows.

Although no sound comes from inside the hut, she knows that her strange guest is suffering untold torment. Since the day she found him– more dead than alive– he has vocalized only once.

She will never forget that sound; an anguish that will mark her for the rest of her days. The wrenching cry of utter agony that tore from the depths of his soul was the audible stain of torment.

He had been tossed onto a refuse pile behind Lord Karpon's keep with the other used goods and garbage. The guards had left him for dead for good reason. They had been long in finishing him.

He should be dead.

She had never seen a man live with such injuries!

His will to survive was strong. He must be young, just entering his prime. . .

Mores the pity.

After the one outburst, he remained silent. *Silent as the forrest before the storm hits.*

Better he screamed out his pain.

Many a day she rode by Karpon's keep– especially when the storerooms were cleaned out. *Useful things could often be found; if one were willing to risk looking for them.* On that particular day she had found a man who was barely alive; a man who had been tossed out like castle refuse.

She wonders how useful he will ultimately prove to be.

On her last trip to the keep– while her guest remained in the hut, shuddering on the bed– she had inadvertently come across some of the palace guards. Karpon's men were cruel and she always tried to avoid them.

As expected, they taunted her, throwing mud just for their sport; laughing as she tried to quickly turn her cart around.

The *safir* beast who pulled the cart pivoted smartly away at her command but the guards still attempted to knock her from her seat. Thankfully, they only used clumps of mud. In the past, they had thrown stones.

As she fled, she noted that both guards were sporting long streamers of what looked to be *hair*. The strands had been knotted to their waistbands.

The locks were not ordinary hair.

The skeins were like nothing she had ever seen before. Silky, long, luxurious. . .

The color was most unusual, as well.

Her guest had come to her nearly scalped; his head bleeding and raw. In the weeks since he had been in the hut, small tufts of hair had started to grow back. The color was so uniquely beautiful that, even now, with its cropped length, it took her breath away.

There could be no other match for *that* hair.

It was the very same strands that the burly guards wore fastened to their waists as a perverted prize. A token of degradation.

They had taken unnatural delight in his destruction!

She swallows down the bile that rises in her throat as the recent memory surfaces. *It must be Familiar hair!* Nothing is said to be as beautiful. *Could he possibly be. . . ?*

Familiars had dual colored eyes. On a few occasions, her guest had tried to open his, but one remained scarred shut.

He probably will never be able to open it.

She wonders if he will ever speak again. *If he can bring himself to speak again.*

Each day she asks him his name; yet each day he remains silent.

The odd thing is that in spite of all of his scars and all his wounds, there are still hints of exceptional *comeliness* to him. It is in the elegant shape of his hands. His impressive height. His overall stature. The glimpses of hair regrowth.

The lush shape of his lips.

In time, most of his physical injuries will heal. But will *he* heal?

The wounds that are visible– horrible though they are– are not as horrible as the wounds the man received to his soul.

She sighs and wipes the sweat from her brow. Would her forrest be enough to heal him? She clutches her healing herbs in a tight grip. The pain of such destruction never lessens!

She knows that first hand.

A tear slips down her weathered cheek.

It pains to see such natural beauty– rare enough on *all* worlds– so blithely destroyed.

On a certain level, this old woman can well appreciate *the concept* of Familiar beauty. It depicts a connection to nature's promise that life, ultimately, is a holy, perfect thing. The natural beauty of the Familiar race is intrinsically a gift of the wild.

But like a light-blade, it comes with two edges.

It reminds some of everything they hope life will encompass: the grace, the splendor, the sensual. Yet, to others, it is a blatant declaration of all they will never have.

Throughout the planets, Familiars were sought after for as many reasons as there were stars in the sky.

And all of these myriad reasons mattered not to these shapeshifters. Steadfastly, they followed paths they alone chose; reminding all– by their very way of life– that true resplendence lies not in their appearance, but in the freedom of their souls.

It is a difficult route for any race to maintain in these troubled times, the old woman acknowledges. She prays she can heal this wounded man for only then will he be free in life to make his own choices.

But. . . how do you heal a man from wounds you can not see?

The loss of the Familiar known as Dariq is greatly mourned on the planet M'yan.

He was a well-loved member of the Mist. A youth on his first adventure. He had held much promise.

But there are many victims these days. Victims of slavers and of Karpon.

The King ordered all Familiar home. The King believes Dariq dead.

No Charl has sensed him. No one will be sent to look for him.

There will be no incarnations for this Familiar. No love. No mate.

Still in his youth, he had not had time to make his true mark upon his people.

Sadly, in time, his name and his existence will fade away much like ink on an ancient page. His memory will be lost inside the complex framework of the life-death struggle all Familiar face.

Nevertheless, the day would come when Dariq's people would surely know his name again.

And the wrath that will come with it.

THE CAT WHO COULD BARK

If there were a thousand spirits
passing by the way
to and fro
in their haste for life–
sidewalks full, feet shuffling,
And a stranger to me, you were
I would still see you.

There is a pure, light beauty
In the soft steps
which belies his pacing
careful and gentle is the tread
that measures its own destiny.
Easy is the stride of unassuming
silence.
So that others mistake
his direction for simple stroll.

If there were a thousand dreams
touching upon my heart
And new to me, yours were
I would still know them.

IN KIRKPATRICK'S WOODS

Every spirit builds itself a house, and beyond its house a world, and beyond its world a heaven. Know then that world exists for you.

-Emerson

He is like the trees that surround her. Tall. Strong. Permanent.

She wonders how he came to be in the middle of the woods— so apart— yet so connected. He never talks of his past so she has no way of knowing. Once she had asked him and he had smiled in his mysterious way. Shrugged his shoulders as if to say 'what possible importance is it?'

It seems as if he has always been here. Rooted.

Yes, he is a "rooted" man.

Her focus falls to his hands. She imagines them in a fresco, somewhere in an ancient ceiling in Italy. The hands speak for him. Sculpted, they convey the masculine embodiment of strength that promises to endure every battle.

They are the hands of artist and subject alike; the eternal prong.

They illustrate the magick he creates. . .

The craft for which he is sought out. He is far removed from city lives and the clackety-crunch of pavement life. Far removed from her.

She has a mind to sleep with him.

Sometimes, at night, she wonders how his sure, capable hands would feel slipping softly over her body. Sometimes she imagines the low, rugged sound of his voice as it rolls over her skin. . . .

"I want you to sleep with me, Kirkpatrick."

Victoria was not sure who was more surprised: her for having blurted her thought out loud– or the man next to her, for having the dubious pleasure of hearing it. Her life was in shambles. She knew it and he knew it.

Duncan Kirkpatrick put his drink down and turned to stare at her in contemplation.

The drink was mulled cider. He made it every evening– rain or shine– so that they could sip the warm, spicy brew as they watched the sun go down over the lake.

The ritual began when she joined him one sunset on his log cabin porch.

He had greeted her with a nod at the steaming mug placed on the empty bentwood rocker next to him. She had always suspected Kirkpatrick had made that chair especially for her. It fit like a glove. When she sat in it to watch the day end in silence with him, it made her feel almost whole for an hour or so.

Yes, for that one hour, she captured the day. The cabin. The lake. Kirkpatrick.

"What did you say?" His voice had the slightest hint of a brogue; Victoria loved listening to it.

The man's hair shifted forward as he faced her. Tussled strands of dark brown and honey that hung almost to his shoulders. When she had first arrived in mid-spring, it was just below his chin. She had since found out that before the spring each year he cut it to chin-length with one easy whack of the scissors.

Throughout all the other seasons, he let it grow.

By winter it cloaked his shoulders.

A rogue's cape for the cold weather.

The color reminded her of trees and woods. It was the shade of dark bark intermingled with lighter shades of honey amber. His hair was interesting and Victoria adored watching the shift and slide of it as he went about his day.

Now he looked at her as if he could not believe what he had heard. Victoria couldn't blame him; their relationship had been defined from day one– they were friends and that was as far as it went.

"I'm just as shocked as you are. I don't know where this-this desire is coming from. As far as I'm concerned, relationships are dead to me. . . but I have to admit. . ."

He raised his eyebrows and waited patiently.

She swallowed. "Sometimes, I watch you from my kitchen window, from across the lake. Especially when you are chopping wood or swimming in the lake. . ." She trailed off, positive she was starting to flush.

He rubbed his chin as he contemplated her bizarre confession.

Victoria's sights fell to his hand. One of the main culprits of her dilemma. *Those beautiful hands. . .*

She cleared her throat. "I don't know where this feeling came from. . ."

That was absolutely true. When she had showed up at his doorstep three months ago, all she wanted was space to clear her muddled thoughts.

She had packed her *stuff* and left New York City for a weekend in Vermont. A few days for a few dollars out in the country to try and regain her life.

She had lost almost all of her savings.

Her money had been invested in the corporate giant that she had done her part to build every day for the past ten years of her life.

The company had cheated clients and workers alike with fanciful bookkeeping and false promises.

The same day they had shut their doors, she had walked into her fiancé's office (the fiancé who was an executive in this same company) only to find out that he had cashed out the previous day and was already on his way to Chile. He informed her in a brief farewell note that extradition would be highly unlikely.

The postscript informed her that he had taken her ring in case he needed extra cash.

The post-postscript suggested that their engagement should probably be broken off, under the circumstances.

Even though Victoria had no idea any of this had been going on , no one wanted to hire an accountant from a Fortune 500 company that was being indicted for misappropriation of funds and for overstating financial sheets.

The upshot was that after ten years of employment she had no references.

That was when Victoria seriously questioned her faith in love, in life and most of all, in herself. Always a strong person, she no longer had faith in faith. How could she be so misled? How could all these people be so misled? Was this end the result of having trust in the nine-to-five? In people? In the doing the right thing?

Where was the karma, dammit!

Confused, disillusioned, (but not bitter) she hit the road; a weekend Kerouac.

She had been driving around the backwoods of Vermont, somewhat lost, when she spotted a small wooden arrow tacked to a tree by the side of the road. It was hanging by a thread. The next good wind would probably knock it down.

It pointed in the direction of a path through the woods just wide enough for a single car. . . .

Victoria learned forward over the steering wheel in an attempt to read the washed-out lettering on the arrow. "Duncan Kirkpatrick, artistry by wood."

An odd sign.

Oddly phrased.

Was the man a painter? Did he use wood in sculpture? Was he the artist or was the wood the artist? What exactly did that damn sign mean?

To people going through hard times, answers to such questions are of paramount importance. It was that need to know that decided her.

She turned her wheel to the left and for the first time in her life, she just followed the road.

The arrow sign had seemed fairly old.

Would the creator of it still be there?

In the middle of the dark way, she had found Kirkpatrick.

A reclusive, brilliant craftsman, whose wooden creations were highly sought after by top galleries and showrooms across the country.

When she arrived, he came out of his workshop and explained to her that he had to finish up a commission for a Danish firm before he could talk to her. He invited her to look around at her leisure while he worked.

Unobtrusively, Victoria walked around, viewing several examples of his work. Since his designs were nothing like the sleek, spare lines of Danish furniture, Victoria was impressed that he had the commission. From what she had seen of his work, form did not always follow function.

The curving lines and twisted branches of his showroom pieces whispered of the beauty of the journey simply for the sake of the adventure.

Kirkpatrick had occasionally observed her, but did not interfere as she combed through the workshop that stood next to a large log house that fronted a private lake.

As the afternoon wore on, Victoria was hesitant to leave the place.

Like the arrow sign, it was odd.

Perhaps she could put the blame on the peace and solitude; the ducks wadding by in the late afternoon, in and out of the dipping branches of willows.

Perhaps it was the utter serenity, the soothing lap of the lake against the shoreline, the pecking of a woodpecker just past the house. . . the sight of Kirkpatrick gently, lovingly, rubbing a magnificent oak table with oils she had watched him mix.

Or perhaps it was simply "the" Kirkpatrick himself– a man who had found his place in the world and lived quietly in it.

He must have sensed her reluctance to leave that day. . . .

"I'm just about done here– Would you like to join me on the porch for some cider?"

She agreed almost too quickly.

He smiled. The corners of moss green eyes crinkled in a way that made Victoria's heart kick. They were ancient eyes. Forrest eyes.

"I should warn you– it's spiked."

"Even better." She smiled back.

As they sat on his porch, watching the sun sink in a rose-banded sky, she had foolishly blurted out her sad tale, blaming 'cider veritas'.

Kirkpatrick had listened silently, letting her stop every now and then as her emotions rose and settled. When she had finished it was full dark.

A firefly zigzagged across the lake like an anime comet. Impossible. Senseless. Spellbinding.

He had taken a sip of his drink, then talked to her in a soft voice. . . .

"Never apologize or bury your sensitivity because of someone else's lack of it. You just need to learn how to trust again." He turned to her. For just an instant there was the most beautiful look in his eyes. . .

He stretched long, jean-clad legs out, rested his bare feet over the edge of the porch railing and crossed them at the ankles. Victoria guessed him to be a man whose seasonal change in clothing would undoubtedly be the same worn out jeans, flannel shirts, and scuffed boots.

"You see that small cabin across the lake from us?"

She nodded.

"It's not much; kinda broken down. Just one room and a bathroom— but the window and the porch face the water. You can take one of the chairs out on the porch and watch the lake whenever you feel like it, rain or shine. Even when you're inside, you can sit by that large window while you read or think or maybe just notice the way the moonbeams fall on the water. It's yours for the summer. If you want it."

Victoria's lips parted like a little girl's. Is he serious?

She blinked. She had just been handed a magnificent present but she was sure it wasn't her birthday. "Okaaay," she drew out the word in disbelief.

"Good." He took a drink of cider.

He was serious. She swallowed.

For some reason, she didn't want to leave this place. *Maybe she could work something out with him? It would be so wonderful to stay here for awhile, free from. . . well, everything.*

"What kind of rent would you charge me because I don't have much —"

"No rent."

Victoria cocked her eyebrow. She wasn't born yesterday. "I wasn't born yesterday. Now seriously, what do you expect out of this if not the rent?"

He exhaled long, slow. Her implication obviously

207

irritated him. "Nothing. I want nothing. I just thought it would be nice to see a human face now and then. The place is empty– you're in need of it. It may help you find your roots again."

She bit her lip, watching him carefully. Assessing him.

He took another sip of his drink. "If you want to come by my porch around sunset every day to share a cider with me, I'd have no objection," he said softly.

"Just a cider?"

It was his turn to cock a brow. "Maybe some conversation. Look, if you are inferring what I think– that's out. I'm not available."

Her cheeks flamed. "I'm sorry, I just thought. . ."

"I'm trying to be decent. I know you don't remember what that's like, having been shagged by Roncom and Mr. Chilean Romance. . ."

He paused to give her a wink.

And, she remembered it had been a very sexy wink.

Not because Kirkpatrick tried; because he didn't.

It was simply the way he was. Homegrown. Earthy. The real thing.

Victoria had accepted his generous offer and spent the first night in the claustrophobic cabin starring out through the curtainless window to the stars.

Apparently he used the cabin for storage. It was loaded with furniture.

She had been cradled by his creativity.

The maple sleigh bed rocked her within its comfortable embrace. She slept for ten straight hours, at peace for the first time in weeks.

She later found out that Kirkpatrick never made similar offers to other people; he was strictly a stay-to-himself kind of man.

So she had been at the cabin for three months.

Shared cider and conversation with him for three months. It was strange, even to her.

And now she had asked him to sleep with her.

"Please don't get bent out of shape about this, Kirkpatrick. I just want to get this. . . whatever. . . *feeling.* . . out of my system. It doesn't seem to want to leave on its own, yet there is nothing out of the ordinary at work here."

"Mmmm." The tip of his finger circled the rim of his mug. Over and over. Victoria became fixated by the motion. "I don't know."

She dragged her attention away from the mug. "About sleeping with me?"

"No. The other comment. I've been told when the situation arises, I can be somewhat out of the ordinary." The man's eyes flashed with glints of humor, turning from moss to forrest green.

"That is, on the odd occasion," he added in an amused tone.

Victoria smiled sheepishly. "I'm sorry. I didn't mean it to sound insulting; I just didn't want you to get the wrong idea."

"Why would I do that?"

"I never thought I would feel this kind of desire again after what Phillip did to me; I guess we are all slaves to the physical after all."

"Not all of us," he murmured wryly.

"Please be serious. Do you think you would want to? Just this one time? I mean, if you don't feel–"

His arm clamped around the back of her neck; he roughly pulled her towards him. "You're an odd duck, Ms. Victoria; d'you know that?"

Lips, warm as summer sunlight, covered hers. The kiss was like the man. Strong and hard and earthy. He tasted of cloves and apples and Kirkpatrick.

He left a permanent impression as complex as the forrest.

If she had been standing her knees would have buckled.

He was more than she had fantasized– and her imagination was highly developed.

He sighed-smiled against her lips, then tilted his head to sample the side of her neck. "That's why I like you." The low voice rasped against her throat, a deep masculine vibration. She almost groaned.

"What are you referring–"

But he never answered her.

His mouth covered hers, his tongue sliding fluidly between her lips. Like hot honey.

His tongue glided over hers, slowly, as if he were savoring each sensation. Each Victoria flavor. The tip stroked against her upper lip, playing with the pliant, rounded softness. Teasing. He dipped into her again and stroked along her upper palate.

Victoria moaned. Was she actually kissing him? The man who had given her shelter from the storm and the space to breath again?

Kirkpatrick– powerful, muscular Kirkpatrick– was as gentle as a summer breeze. And he kissed more like artist than woodsman. Yet his strong grip bespoke a man living off the land in harmony with nature. His muscles were the result of a hard day's work and not a Nautilus.

There is something indefinably different about him. . .

210

Kirkpatrick had fascinated her from the first day she had met him. Victoria had more questions than she had answers about him. She supposed he was just that kind of man.

The kind you never figure out.

In an odd way, he reminded her of her aunt's recipes. They were delicious; but there was always one ingredient that she could never quite name. That elusive ingredient was what gave the dish its magic. Elevated the mundane to the sublime.

Kirkpatrick was an elusive ingredient.

In these woods. In her life.

Victoria longed for more than a sample of him.

Her tongue toyed with his, darting against his, until he allowed her to enter his mouth. She got the impression he did not allow many these kinds of privileges.

And he *was* a privilege to explore, to experience.

Her fingers twined in his hair, tugging at the long locks. The strands were shiny-smooth. Even as she kissed him, she could discern its clean, crisp scent; it always reminded her of the tangy spices of mulled cider.

The scent evoked images of a fresh walk in an autumn forrest.

He sighed into her mouth, the faintest, rawest sound of pleasure. It was the sexiest vocal expression she had every heard any man utter.

She shivered.

"What is it? Are you cold?" He laved the corner of her lips with the warm tip of his tongue.

Cold? How could she be cold wrapped inside the arms of such a man? "No. . . just. . ."

But she couldn't finish because his large hands– warm

and sure– were stroking up and down her back. Heating her. Caressing her.

His touch felt so wonderful that she had no way to answer him.

She didn't have to.

He murmured in her ear. "Maybe it is the warmth that chills you. . ."

Victoria did not deny it.

Her intention had been to come over for apple cider. Nothing more. At least nothing consciously more.

Her washed-out sleeveless shirt with its long row of tiny buttons didn't seem much like seducing material, but the sure hands that moved reverently over the small discs, undoing them, treated the frayed madras as if it was an altar cloth.

The edges of her mouth tilted in an ironic grin. "You like plaid, Kirkpatrick?"

Moss-colored eyes met hers. A twinkle of Celtic humor laced with desire. "Aye, I like plaid fine enough." He winked at her in the lazy manner that had been getting prime Scottish rogues in trouble for centuries.

She laughed. The crystalline sound danced across the night waters of his lake.

An owl hooted in response.

"Now don't be getting too serious on me, Ms. Victoria." He grinned, keeping the mood light. Two curving laugh lines scored his cheeks. His palm brushed over her collarbone, feathering up the side of her throat.

"I would never get serious with a woodsman the likes of you, Kirkpatrick."

He reached down with both hands to cup her behind, lifting her onto the porch railing. He titled his rocker, coming close to her. "Don't make promises you can't keep."

Seated in front of him like this, she was positioned a head higher than him. For potential play, the placement was rather clever. She gave him high marks for inventiveness.

Victoria had not associated his artistic creativity to potential sexual inventiveness. The man was so damn subtle. In the one move, he had shown her that she had overlooked an important facet of his nature.

His lovemaking might prove to be uncommon.

She had often watched him as he worked; there was always an intensity to him. He blocked out the world. He fell into the design, lost in the curves and hollows he created.

Would he make love the same way?

Suddenly she *had* to know.

And with that realization came another.

She was not sure why Kirkpatrick had told her he was unavailable on the day she had met him. Was he simply trying to ease her concerns? In the three months she had been at the lake, he had not had one woman there socially. For a man who looked like he did, it was surely by choice–Kirkpatrick was one sexy beast.

Once, she even had joked to him about his lack of intimate relationships. He had simply replied, "It is not the right season for it."

She wasn't sure if he was serious or not.

One thing was certain, he had never been less than a perfect gentleman. The man lived to the notes of nature. Different, but true.

She wanted to know Kirkpatrick one time before she left these woods forever.

One time to get the desire out of her system.

If she didn't, she knew she would wonder about him for the rest of her life. There were very few men who inspired that kind of wonder or desire in her.

Kirkpatrick shifted his focus to her gaping shirt. Moonlight lathered the skin of her chest and midriff to a silvery sheen. Her bra looked impossibly white in the glow. Like the item in the commercials that had been washed in Tide and not 'that other detergent'.

The absurdity of the human mind at times like this. She laughed softly at herself.

"Want to share?"

She shook her head. "You'll think I'm whacked."

He clicked his tongue. "I already think your whacked." His fingers stroked the side of her face, his knuckles lightly skimming over her breastbone, down the center of her chest over the bra clasp, and down to her midriff.

His hands feel so hot. Almost electric.

As was his way, he didn't press her for a response.

Which was the reason she decided to tell him. "My bra looks bizarre–that's all."

"Really?" He cocked his head to the side, examining the object in question. Or more precisely the mounds held in check by the object. "How do you figure that now?"

She shrugged her shoulders. "I don't know; it looks irradiated or something under this light. . ."

Kirkpatrick gave her a steady stare. "Actually, let me correct myself. You are definitely more whacked than I gave you credit for." He grinned suddenly, flashing white teeth at her.

Victoria noted that his teeth did not look irradiated–just beautiful. No bleached piano key look for this man.

Beautiful, naturally white teeth.

How will those teeth feel scraping over my body. . . She flushed. She hadn't been with anyone since Phillip.

He keenly observed her reaction. "Are you sure you're ready for this?"

"I've been ready for a long time."

His eyes glazed over with a sheen that she interpreted as desire.

"Good. That's good." He bent forward and soon his lips retraced the path of his fingers. His mouth was like a velvet petal drifting over her skin.

The tender kisses gave way to tiny nips. He rubbed his face against her breasts and Victoria's hands sunk into his hair. He captured her nipple through her silk bra, tugging at the hardened peak.

Kirkpatrick's fingers, which had been softly stroking the skin at her waist, stilled when she trembled. "I think you are cold."

Before she could respond, strong, carpenter's hands clasped her sides. He effortlessly brought her over onto his lap.

His legs were a solid, muscular support.

With his strong arms around her she was cradled in the most perfect haven. He was the kind of man who liked washed out flannel shirts with rolled up sleeves. She had never *ever* dated a man who had that kind of fashion sense. Her past men were of the Armani persuasion.

She rested her head against his chest; her short, dark gel-spiked hair poked right through the worn material of his shirt. Victoria had cut off all her hair when she had lost her job. It had taken ten years to grow below her waist. The exact same amount of life that she had given to the company.

Kirkpatrick ran the flat of his palm over the spikes which were sticking straight up on the top of her head. She imagined she felt like a hedgehog.

He seemed to like it, though. He kept running his fingers back and forth over the scrub-brush. The repetitive motion was oddly soothing and slightly stimulating.

"I suppose it was stupid to hack off my hair like that."

"We all have our reasons for doing things. Yours was more. . ." His lips turned up at the conners. ". . . *declamatory* than most. But still nothing to feel sorry about."

She sighed. "It looks terrible."

"You turned yourself into a phoenix, Victoria. I think that's rather beautiful."

If she had let them, her eyes would have filled with tears. Kirkpatrick had a way of seeing a person. *Inside.* Sometimes she wondered if he looked at her as he did the wood he worked with day by day. She wondered what his mind's eye fashioned out of her.

She was no artistic creation and never would be.

Yet. . . artists saw art where others didn't.

Perhaps she was just being fanciful on this moonlit night on the lap of a ruggedly handsome man.

"Let's see what this phoenix will reveal. . ." His teeth caught at the front catch of her bra. Somehow– she wasn't sure how– the bra was undone, she felt the moist slide of his tongue between the valley of her breasts.

He was very practiced. Another surprise.

Wide palms flattened on her back just above her waist, under the thin material of her shirt. He brought her tight up against him, burying his face in the valley between her breasts.

There, he inhaled deeply of her scent– only to glance up at her, catching her off guard in that moment.

The perfect feel of his mouth, his administrations, had her head falling back slightly, her eyelids heavy.

A corner of his mouth lifted in satisfaction as he watched her silently.

She brushed his hair back from his face, gliding her fingers deep into the thick locks. He stilled, clearly surprised.

"What is it?" she whispered.

"You are part of this magnificent painting before me, Victoria– the lake, the moonlight, you on my lap, your head thrown back, the sensual expression on your face. It is as if you were part of these woods forever. Part of, one with. Elemental Earth and elemental female. Moon and water. Like the ancient legends. . ."

"What legends?"

A shutter came over him. He seemed to fall into his own thoughts. "I wish I was a painter then I could capture you and you would stay this way, forever on the brink. Canvas is so fixed a medium, though, isn't it? I deal with the opposite. I deal with change. Trees are a living, growing medium. . . "

Was this Kirkpatrick speaking? The distant, reclusive, woodsman? It sounded more like the words of an artist or a poet. He was a raw, sexy kind of guy. . . but romantic?

Who'd have thunk it?

Victoria gave him an ironic look. "Are you sure you're not part Irish?"

His laughter rolled low in this throat, the vibration surging over her. She discovered that a man's laughter felt good when it tickled your skin.

His fingers flicked back and forth over the breasts he had just kissed. "I'll become Irish when these become blarney stones, lass."

She snickered and shook her finger at him.

He winked at her.

Smiling, Victoria bent over him, her hands tangled in his long hair. "I think you're going to turn out to be quite a handful."

A dimple grooved his cheek. His brogue became noticeably thicker. "Only if we're both *verra* lucky, Victoria."

She laughed again. His light banter was putting her at ease in what might have been an awkward situation. But then, he had always known how to soothe her.

As he held her closer to him, his hands slid higher up on her back. He placed his lips just beneath her throat, right in the well of her collarbone. He opened his mouth on that spot, drawing deeply as his tongue made her tingle with tiny flicks. The sensations traveled, zinging through her entire body.

Suddenly, he effortlessly lifted her back up onto the cool porch railing. "Don't worry, I intend to keep you warm."

A rather sexy promise from a man. She liked it.

Two strong hands cupped her buttocks, gently kneading. It flashed though Victoria's mind that at some point Kirkpatrick might not be gentle. He was too raw a man for that.

She imagined that if the occasion was right he could be deliciously rough.

She hoped this one time they were together, she would get a taste of that kind of wild passion; she had never experienced it before. *Raw sex.*

Once she had seen a production of a Tennessee Williams play in summer stock. The production was so-so; except for the lead actor. *He* was spectacular. Exuding hot, sweaty Southern-boy charm, he had that jutted hipbone, lazy kind of strut that spilled testosterone all over the stage. Her date had dissed the production; she had gone into high octane for the rest of the night.

Even though he was not an overheated Southern boy, Kirkpatrick had that same quality. Barefoot, in washed out jeans and an over-washed flannel shirt, the man was steam heat.

With his arms on both sides of her, his palms inched beneath the waistband of her shorts, dipping over the rounded globes of her buttocks. She hadn't bother to put on any underwear beneath her shorts.

The tips of his fingers pressed into the supple flesh. He inched lower until she was almost sitting on his hands.

As he did this, his mouth rubbed against hers back and forth, his breath, sweetly scented by the cider spices.

The simple movements were so erotic and so Kirkpatrick.

She inhaled a long, ragged breath of air, and tried to keep still.

This was an entirely new situation for her.

Normally she was a very aggressive partner; but she had thrown the ball in his court, so to speak. It was up to him to lob it back.

By unspoken acknowledgment, it seemed only right that he set the pace. She had invited him to come and get it.

He played with the corner of her mouth then caught her lower lip between his teeth and suckled on it. He did the same with her upper lip– only this time one of his fingers snaked up between her buttocks to slide against her cleft.

Then he began licking the center of her upper lip; his tongue toying with its pliant fullness. It felt incredibly good. Bands of pleasure flowed over her. To prolong the sensation Victoria sat straighter up on the rail and arched into his finger.

Bending forward, she pursed her lips and blew a cool stream of breath, riffling the long strands along the side of his head, over and around his ear. Then she changed her breath, exhaling straight from her diaphragm; a sultry, streaming caress to his throat and earlobe.

He shivered in her arms.

It was a heady experience to feel a rough-and-tumble man like him shake with desire. When she nibbled at his ear, her tongue darted playfully in the folds. A damp little tickle.

He trembled again.

"Have I found your Achilles spot?" She barely spoke above a whisper.

He still heard her.

"The question is," he spoke into her chest as he rubbed his chin along the plump edge of her breast, ". . .rather moot." With that cryptic response, he took her breast into his mouth and suckled hard on the jutting peak.

Victoria reared up off the bannister, her groan of pleasure acknowledged by the movement of his hands beneath her. The edge of his palm skated over the crease of her bottom, edging between the globes.

Victoria froze for a moment, surprised by the erotic gesture. "Oh! . . .um. . ."

He smiled against her nipple, rolling the protruding tip between his teeth.

Again the thought flickered across her mind:

Kirkpatrick is highly skilled. She had imagined that his lovemaking would be pretty good. Honest, straight forward sex. Pleasurable and fulfilling. His adept moves, however, indicated complexity. *Where had he been before he came to this forrest?*

In the time she had been here, she had not been able to find out any information about him. The nearest town was ten miles away and no one there seemed to know anything about him either. She went into town at least once a week for supplies and to visit the local nursery.

The few times she had broached the subject she was met with closed, blank stares. Of course New Englanders– especially country people– were generally closed-off to 'outsiders' until a certain amount of trust developed.

Usually that took about thirty years.

She had been around a mere three months.

She had only met one person in town that she considered somewhat friendly. Kathy Beringer owned several lovely Victorian shops. She had seen Kathy's larger shop in Bennington earlier on, so had made it a point to visit the smaller one in the local village. Kathy often came by the valley shop as it was her first place of business. Their conversations were friendly, albeit brief.

The only response she ever got from Kathy was surprise that she was staying in such primitive surroundings. (That was Kathy's label, not hers.) Victoria thought the place was beautiful.

Kirkpatrick's free hand encircled her waist and brought her out of her reverie. He deftly unbuttoned the top button of her shorts making quick work of the zipper as well.

He glanced down to the gaping material where her dark curls glistened. They were slick with dew.

"No spell could ever be as enchanting. . ."

Soon his fingers tangled in the tiny curls, sinking into the warm, velvety mound. He kneaded the firm flesh. His hand became covered with her slick fluid. The heel of his palm pressed above her pubic bone, massaging her in circular motions as his fingers continued to stroke her.

Victoria clutched his broad shoulders. A slight breeze cooled the back of her neck but the rest of her was on *fire*.

Bringing his fingers to his mouth, he licked the taste of her off of them. By the light of the moon, she could see the pupils of his moss-colored eyes dilate, then glaze over with desire. His heartbeat thundered against her, ripples of energy that seemed to augment her excitement for him with each surging pulse.

Before she knew it, he pulled her shorts down her legs, casting them to the wooden plank floor. She sat on the rail with nothing covering her but an open shirt and moonlight.

Kirkpatrick sat back in the rocker. Folding his hands together, he tapped the tips of his thumbs against one another. He caught her eye and simply stared at her.

Still breathing raggedly from his ministrations, Victoria's mouth parted slightly. *Why had he stop-ped? What was he doing?*

He began to rock back and forth in the rocker. Slowly. Never breaking eye contact with her. His thumbs tapping to the same beat.

His stare burned into her.

She wondered what had caused this intensity in him. Desire? Anger? Or was it just simply the way he always made love?

The same way he made his furniture.

She had seen him work; he poured all of himself into the

task. She supposed it went part and parcel with the creative nature. Victoria had never thought about that while she had lusted after his body.

Kirkpatrick would never do anything halfway.

She swallowed as he continued to pin her with heated eyes.

In the stillness of the night the sexual tension mounted with each roll of the chair runners.

"Open your legs."

She gasped slightly. True, she had put herself in this position– she just hadn't counted on a full metal response. While she wasn't exactly a shy person, she was never one to put herself on display.

With him looking at her like this, she felt unaccountably, traditionally shy. She cleared her throat.

"I. . . ah, I. . ."

A line grooved into the right side of his face giving him an impossibly roguish look. Once again he had shifted the tone on her. "Stop dilly-dallying and open your legs, Ms. Victoria."

So she did.

And still he just watched her.

She managed to keep her ground even though she was, well, unsettled about being seen– *really seen*– in this manner.

He steepled his index fingers and rested his chin upon the tips. He rocked the chair slowly. Victoria noted the *creak. . .* pause. . . *creak* of the runners against the wooden floor.

The sound was strangely hypnotic.

Gradually, he gazed up at her, meeting her embarrassed yet brave stare.

"Initially you came to me to hide, Victoria. But you can't hide. Even here, in the middle of the woods, you must eventually come to show yourself."

She viewed him curiously.

"The thing is to be certain that those you expose yourself to in life are those that can truly appreciate the view."

Her cheeks flamed in outrage. "So is that what this was? A lesson in life from the wise woodsman?" Her hand swept down to snatch up her shorts. "You never had any intention of sleeping with me, did you?"

His hand clamped over her wrist, stilling her. *"Like hell I don't."*

In the few seconds it took to digest his words he had already unzipped his jeans. His erect member jutted through the opening. Long, thick, hard. The vein on the sides throbbed– the pulse beat reminded her of his rocking.

She starred at him.

The moonlight captured a droplet of glistening moisture as it rolled off the head. He was more affected by her than his outward demeanor let on.

She wanted him all the more.

His hands clasped her waist, lifting her. Then, he suddenly stopped.

"It seems I am about to take a great leap of faith here– and so are you. I assume you are protected in this?"

She swallowed and nodded shortly. "Wh-what about you?"

He snorted. "Are you serious? I live like a friggin' monk up here."

Without further ado, he sunk into her fast. Impaling her. *And he went deep.*

"Duncan!"

Victoria rarely used his first name. She supposed it was her way of keeping a distance between them.

Well, there was no distance between them now.

Not even a millimeter.

'Yes, Vicki, I'm *here.*" His low voice feathered the shell of her ear. Soothing. *Hot.*

He began to thrust in her. Long, measured strokes– again, like the rocker. Up and down. In and out. He filled her so completely that she shuddered. Not in release but in acceptance.

He was right, after the fiasco with Roncom, she had cut herself off from everything in life.

She has lost her way, her values, her desire. She spends long hours questioning what is happening in this country. Is Roncon a true symbol for twenty-first century capitalism? Or is it just the bad seed. Is this where we are going? What has gone so horribly wrong?

Maybe Roncom lost it way, like she has; defiled by men whose selfishness knows no bounds? She believed in this society; she believed in the strength of our dollars. Dollars which are inscribed with the words: "In God we Trust". She thinks that the words are put there to signify that decency is our equal partner– our higher conscience in a society that sometimes seems to be built on the principle that making money is the reason d'etre.

Until this moment she doesn't realize how deeply her foundations are damaged in this "just" business world solely compromised of mile after mile of money metropolises, this sea of megalithic Roncons. What happened to the souls of those corporate leaders? Did they ever have souls?

Or were they an army of dopplegangers, cardboard replacements who waved the posters of what we used to be in our faces? They didn't get paid for their humanity. But then, who did? Twisting words until euphemism begot euphemism.

Open was closed.

Profit was loss.

And decency had drowned; its last gasp stamped out by the footprint of More.

So Kirkpatrick is right.

She has come here to hide.

And somehow she is finding herself in a man who makes his living by hand.

It is the way this county was built.

Can she find that idealistic part of herself once again in him and his way of life? She doesn't know. . . But she feels alive once more.

He feels alive.

And so good! Everything about him is good. Who he is as a person, his way of living, the energy he pours into everything he does.

He is a woodsman, a quintessential American man. Unique in himself. Sure about his beliefs. He carries his Scots heritage with him and you could never sell him the Brooklyn bridge. . . .

Kirkpatrick surged up into her as strong and swift as the tides that come upon our shores from sea to shining sea.

He began to rock.

Back and forth, he moved the chair, tensing, flexing his thigh muscles. His breathing was stronger, a sheen of sweat glimmered on his brow. Yet she knew Kirkpatrick would stay the course. He was a man who would see every battle to the end.

The motion of the chair augmented his thrusts, adding depth, adding pleasure. Victoria moaned, kissing him on the mouth. A beautiful, deep kiss. He was going to ride her home.

He flexed inside her. She could feel him throbbing, swelling larger. He rocked her faster. Shivers scorched her body.

"Duncan, please, please. . . !"

"What you want you must first give to yourself," he whispered, hoarsely.

"I- I don't know what you mean."

He took her wrist, moved her hand down to the juncture where they joined.

Bleary-eyed, she gazed at him, not sure what he wanted of her.

His fingers wrapped over hers, guiding them between her cleft to where they slid over him, against her, as he drove in and out of her.

The added friction combined with his movements and the increased rocking sent her over the edge.

Screaming her release, she tumbled into pleasure; her contractions clamping around their entwined fingers. Around his shaft.

When Kirkpatrick knew she had come, only then would he find his own release. Locking her to him, he poured hot and heavy into her.

She fell forward, he fell back in the rocker, spent, out-of-breath.

The moon was full over the lake now. Frogs were

croaking, crickets were chirping, Kirkpatrick's wind chimes clinked in the light breeze.

They stayed silent, absorbing the night and what had transpired between them. Two strangers who had become friends and were now lovers.

"Stay the night with me." His lips idly grazed her earlobe. "I'll make you pancakes in the morning."

Victoria stilled. Complication was the last thing she needed.

"I can't. This was not about me staying the night, Kirkpatrick. I told you that."

He exhaled heavily. "It's about getting me out of your system?"

"Yes."

"You're right, then. So don't stay the night. But you can still come by and have pancakes in the morning."

She laughed. He always had the amazing ability to say just the right thing at right time. Not too many men could make that claim.

He smiled down at her.

Then he began to rock again.

Slowly and evenly.

Victoria's next remark caught in her throat. She was feeling him harden inside her.

"Duncan?" Her voice came out unsure, thin.

"Mmmm."

"We said one time, Duncan. *One time.*"

The sexy, lopsided grin he gave was pure Scottish rake. "This does not count as a separate event, Ms. Victoria; I haven't disengaged yet." He flexed inside her to punctuate his point.

Victoria snorted– then sucked in her breath as he rapidly

swelled, making the fit very tight. "This time around," he murmured huskily, "I'll do it all for you."

And didn't he just.

He looks up from his drawing and sees her through his window. The door to her cabin opens, then closes. He waits a few minutes. The door opens again. She walks outside and makes it halfway around the lake before turning back.

He watches her until the door closes then resumes his sketch. He is starting a new project tomorrow; today he will finish his initial plans. The drawing will be sketchy; he will let his inspiration guide him as the work is being done...

It wasn't until late afternoon that Victoria finally made her way around the lake.

Over and over, she had tried to talk herself out of the trip to the other side of the forrest. She had not gone over to his place in the morning for pancakes.

Or anything else.

For one thing, she wasn't sure Kirkpatrick had been serious about the offer.

Even if he was, she was not sure she should accept.

One time she had told him. To get him out of her system.

But, he wasn't out of her system.

In fact, she couldn't stop thinking about him. The way he felt sliding against her, in her. His musky, clean scent. The incomparable method of his touch when he drew her in to his arms.

That morning he had come out onto his porch, sat in the

same rocker they had made love in the previous night, and ate a huge plate of pancakes. The whopping dish balanced precariously on his lap.

By the size of the stack he had indeed made extra for her.

She had actually set out one time, but turned back.

She just couldn't bring herself to go across the entire distance to the other side.

So Kirkpatrick ate his solitary breakfast on the porch. During the entire time he never once glanced at her cabin.

By mid-afternoon, Victoria finally convinced herself she was being too stupid to live. The man *did* something to her. Last night's exercise in spiced *steam-rocking* had not doused the fire.

To the contrary. It felt as though gasoline had been poured over licking flames.

Finally admitting to herself that she still had a thirst for the carpenter and that thirst needed to be quenched one more time in order to be satisfied, she actually trudged the rest of the way around the lake to his cabin.

Kirkpatrick was around the side, planing and cutting wood. His green shirt had been flung over a low branch of a tree.

Out of his line of sight, she took the opportunity to observe him as he worked.

Beads of moisture trickled down his muscular torso, delineating its planes and curves with the sheen of a working man's sweat. Blue jeans tightened around lean hips and rock-solid thighs as he bent forward with each and every stroke of the labor-intensive task.

He straightened suddenly and flung his hair back, out of his eyes. Then he wiped the dampness from his brow with the edge of his forearm. Kirkpatrick didn't turn around, but he knew she was there.

And he didn't seem surprised.

"I'm almost done. I'll just be a minute." His voice was laced with that sexy, rough quality that some men get when they are doing physical labor.

Of any kind.

The man felled his own trees; cut and planed the wood himself. Throughout the summer Victoria had watched him get in his pickup and head out into the woods. It usually took him a day, sometimes two, to get the specific properties of wood he wanted for individual pieces.

She continued to observe him. Once again, he bent low over a long piece of lumber, this time following the path of the grain with the sander he was using. Victoria recognized this wood; he had told her it was for a cabinet he was working on for a local doctor. The piece was being fashioned out of Cherry wood. Hundreds of hours had already gone into designing and making it.

With one last swipe of the sander, Kirkpatrick passed his hand over the plank. His work was perfection and he took pride in what he handcrafted.

As he reached for his shirt hanging over the tree limb, he glanced at her over his shoulder. Clearly, he was waiting for her to say something.

All she could seem to do was stand and stare at him. Wide-eyed. Not sure what to say. . . *except that she wanted him one more time.*

Last night in the rocking chair, he had held her for hours. Kept her warm against the night breeze. . .

Because she wouldn't come inside to stay the night.

Because she couldn't get herself to leave the security of

his comforting embrace.

She had slipped away when he finally went inside to get a blanket for them.

A coward's way out to be sure. But cleaner. For both of them.

She ran her palms down the front of her thighs, nervous. "You were right, Kirkpatrick."

He gave her a crooked grin. "I'm always right. But what exactly are you referring to, Ms. Victoria?"

Many times, when she called him Kirkpatrick, he responded by referring to her as Ms. Victoria. She was not sure why, but his eyes always danced with amusement. Even though they had known each other all summer and they had been together last night, she could not bring herself to call him Duncan.

Duncan was too close, too personal. Duncan was a name she had always particularly liked.

Had she called him that last night in the throes of their lovemaking? She could not remember. . .

His moss-colored eyes examined her from head to bare foot.

For some stupid reason she tried to hide her big toe behind her left ankle. The corners of his lips lifted in private reverie– as if her action had revealed something about her. Something he liked.

She stood up straighter and cleared her throat. "I should have stayed the night."

"Really," he drawled, wiping the back of his neck with his balled-up shirt. "And why is that?"

Victoria lifted her chin. He never made anything easy. "To see if you snore, Kirkpatrick."

He laughed, low, rich. His eyes were filled with fire.

"Why would you want to know?"

"Snoring would break the spell- take you completely out of my system. Just-like-that." She snapped her fingers.

He arched his eyebrow. "Did you say *spell*?"

Perhaps she had gone too far? She swallowed. "Well, in a sense."

"In a sense." He tossed his shirt over his shoulder and began to advance on her. By the determined look on his face, he was not going to engage in further small talk.

"*Yes.*"

His molten expression told her he was remembering every nuance of their time last night. Every shiver. Every sigh.

She swore she could feel his body heat rise as he approached her. "Y-yes?"

He backed her right into his workshop. Right up against a perfectly planed maple table.

"*Hell, yes.*"

He glanced down at the long georgette skirt she had put on that day. With its loose, flowing material, it was more like a slip. Victoria loved it because it felt so light; she loved the feel of the silk as it drifted freely about her legs when she walked. It made her think of exotic places, where island breezes played against impossibly interesting women; women who, unlike her, knew how to make men slaves to their magic. . .

Not bad for a skirt she purchased at an off-price store.

Kirkpatrick seemed to know her mood; his gaze became passion-drugged.

Without a word, his hands clasped her waist in a strong grip. Before she blinked, he effortlessly lifted her onto the table.

Victoria fell back against the smooth, cool wood. Like a

palm leaf shifting in the wind.

Kirkpatrick slid his hands under that silken wisp of a skirt and smoothly slid her panties down her legs. His fingertips trailed after like streaks of butter melting against her skin.

It felt too good for her own good.

Victoria raised herself up on her elbows as he came over her.

"Aren't you being presumptuous?"

"Don't think so." He tossed her underwear over his shoulder as he unbuttoned the top button of his jeans.

"Hmmm."

"By the way. . ." He slowly slid the tab of the zipper over the metal teeth. Inch by inch, his dusky skin was revealed to her– and then, the beautiful, rigid length of his manhood. "In fairness to your desire to get me out of your system, I feel I should tell you something."

She dragged her sights away from the captivating display and met his penetrating look with one of apprehensive curiosity. "And what is that?"

"I don't snore, Victoria."

With that warning, he pulled her tightly to him.

The debate ended with the first, swift thrust.

Hard and sure as a carpenter's hands.

She feels him enter her. . . sliding in and out. . . he withdraws and rubs the tip of his member over her clitoris. . . sinking into her again. . . and again and again. . . until all she focuses on is his penetration and thrusts. . . but he swiftly withdraws, changes position. . . his mouth slides between her legs. . . his tongue is sizzling, licking, drawing.

234

. . she is so wet, that she pours all over his face. . . she calls out his name. . . he moves again. . . now he enters her to the fullest depths. . . he is so heavy, so rigid. . . his manhood drives into her dewy folds. . . his wide palms lift her bottom up to meet his thrusts. . . she reaches for him but it is his mouth that is working on her again. . . his teeth scrape over her sensitized skin. . . he blows cool air over her. . . he laps her hot. . . he brings her to the edge of oblivion. . . again and again. . . lightening charges the room as a summer storm breaks overhead. . . he stops to change how he comes to her. . . he thrusts in her again. . . she wants to scream. . . she does scream.

Victoria spent that night with Duncan Kirkpatrick.

He kept her warm, wrapping her with himself.

Twice during the night they made love.

She wasn't sure but she had a sinking suspicion that she had been the one to initiate the encounters; both of which had been wild explosions of passion.

The next morning, his arms made a futile attempt to pin her to the mattress as she jumped out of bed.

There was nothing said between them as she put on her clothes.

Kirkpatrick rolled over onto his stomach and slammed the pillow over his head.

Later in the afternoon he came looking for her. She was sitting in the small front room.

He knocked on the wood-framed screen door even though Victoria gave him a good impression of a woman reading a book. She had been staring at the same page for thirty-five minutes.

She had been thinking about him.

About being intimate with him.

The way he touched her. The silent reverence in his caress. The endearingly crooked smile he gave her after the second time they had made love. . .

She tried to act nonchalant when she glanced up to see him standing at the door. Of course her heart skipped a beat. She had wanted him the first day she had met him.

And maybe unconsciously before that.

Desire is a fantastical beast, isn't it?

Now that she slept with him, just looking at him, thinking of him, made her want to experience him anew.

"Are you busy?"

"No-no. I was just reading." She pushed back a lock of her hair. Unfortunately it wasn't there since she cut it all off.

Her hand kind of faltered in midair.

Kirkpatrick noticed, of course. His secret smile told her that.

"Did you need something?" Her face immediately flamed at the poor choice of words.

"I don't think I can actually answer that." He grinned. "Except to say I came by to see if you would like to come with me today?

"What?"

I'm starting a new project and I need to go get some wood, Victoria."

Kirkpatrick had never asked her to go with him on a wood hunt. She knew that he was very particular about the wood he used. She was curious as to how he went about finding it.

"I would like to see that."

"Would you?" His eyes were brimming with laughter.

And Victoria knew why. "I just asked to see some wood, didn't I?"

"Uhuh."

"After you asked me to come with you."

"Uhuh."

She closed her book and set it on the table next to her. "Well, can I go like this?"

His assessing gaze traveled the length of her. She was wearing shorts and a tee. "It's up to you. I think you're fine—coming and going; but you might want to change into long pants to cover your legs for protection."

"Ok, give me a minute."

He nodded. "I'll meet you up by the tractor."

Victoria watched the tree line by the dirt road as Kirkpatrick maneuvered his tractor through the wooded area.

He had hitched a trailer to the back of the tractor. They were deep into the forrest primeval, following a dirt path.

She straddled his left knee, precariously balanced. To keep her steady, Kirkpatrick held her with his left arm as he drove.

"What are we looking for?"

"This is a special design. I need just the *right* kind of wood."

"What kind would that be?"

"The kind that feels right."

"The kind that feels right. O-KAY. Clear as mud." He nudged her bottom with his knee, making her bob up and down.

"You know. . . it has to feel right. . . *like last night*." He brushed his chin along the back of her neck. The warmth of his breath tingled the skin at the back of her collar.

Victoria shivered a little. She had not expected him to be a man that did such things– so when he did the results were potent. The woodsman was proving to be a sensualist, with all the right, rough edges.

Kirkpatrick leaned forward over the steering wheel as if he were picking up invisible signals from the trees themselves. Victoria started laughing.

"What?" He turned to her with a grin.

"Are you in some kind of Vulcan mind meld with the forrest?"

His grin deepened. "You'd be surprised." He nipped her earlobe, his teeth catching on the rim, tugging.

Her heart jumped a beat. The spot between her legs took a beat. And moistened.

To give merit to his patented behavior of seek-and-search, he unexpectedly pulled up the tractor and cut the engine.

Victoria looked at him inquiringly.

"We walk from here."

"This is the spot?" She waved her hand through the air. The place they were located seemed much the same as any other area they had passed along the trail. Trees, bushes, forrest.

"Yes."

"Hmmm. Okay."

"Can you get to the step or do you want me to lift you over?"

"I think I can do it."

Kirkpatrick sat back, calmly watching her descent. In order to get off of his leg, her behind had to rub the length of his thigh. A slight gleam lit his eyes but as usual he was contained.

The only time she had ever seen him not contained was when he made love. There was so much passion within him...

Victoria was doing pretty good getting down, even with her errant thoughts– until she realized she was facing the wrong way. Her foot froze midair, hovering somewhere above the step.

"I guess I should've have turned around."

"Yep."

"I just-*oh*!" Before she added another word he neatly lifted and turned her in the air.

Duncan Kirkpatrick was a very strong man.

"Okay now?" He drawled, his mouth just inches from her own.

Victoria stared up at him. He was a Marlboro man (plenty of smoke without the cigarettes) yet whenever she tried to figure out logically what it was about him that melted and burned her feminist insides to licking flames of 'gotta have him', she never could quite get it.

But her body got it.

Yes indeedy; it did.

Victoria wiped her damp palms on her jeans. "All right, Mr. Bunyan. What now?"

He jumped down next to her, his Wolverine work boots sending up clouds of dust.

"Now, Ms. Victoria, we walk."

"*Walk*?" As if she never heard of such a thing before.

"You know. . . that's where you put your two feet together then separate them by rubbing your thighs back and forth against each other." He cocked his head to the side. "Kind of like what you did last night– except with no forward motion and no loud moaning."

Her mouth dropped open. And her cheeks burned at the rather accurate description.

Grabbing his tool pack, he took her hand and boldly led her into the forrest. Her sneakers and his work boots crunched over pine needles, dead leaves, twigs. The sounds were somehow soothing.

Just ahead a fallen branch blocked their path.

Kirkpatrick knelt down in front of it. The leaves were still alive, so the branch had fallen recently. "It was sheared off by the lightening last night."

Victoria glanced around the woods. "There doesn't seem to be a lot of damage from the storm."

"No. Just this limb so far. A nice healthy limb. . ." He ran his hand reverently over the bark. "Stand back a little; I'm going to strip some of these smaller branches away."

"You're taking it for your project?"

"I'm taking it, but not for that project." He reached around to his pack. Pulling out some worn leather work gloves, goggles, and a small machete, he began to hack off branches and strip off leaves.

Victoria knelt down to watch him work, carefully staying out of range of the machete. "What will you use it for?"

He hesitated slightly. "Picture frames, I think. Good carving wood."

She chuckled. It was the last thing she expected to hear. "Why picture frames, of all things?"

"This limb was sheared off from its parent tree. Separated from its home, you might say. In its next life, it can hold pictures of families and loved ones. Yeah, it will do nicely with that," he remarked absently. "That's a perfect transition."

Victoria gave him an oblique look. "Kirkpatrick, let me rephrase what you just. . . I mean, you sound as if there is an actual spirit inside the wood and this living spirit goes into the things you make. Have you been living out here by yourself too long, do you think?"

He paused, then glanced briefly at her over his arm. "Sometimes you just have to do what feels right, Victoria."

She had been joking. She was not so sure he was. "You can't actually believe trees have spirits?"

He shrugged.

"Isn't that rather Celtic of you, Kirkpatrick?"

He winked at her through the goggles.

"You know, you continually amaze me."

His eyes met hers. Suddenly as green as the leaves around them. Clear and serious.

What is he thinking? she wondered– as she had so many times throughout the summer. *He is so like the woods*, she realized. Dark at times. Deep. *Easy to get lost in. . .*

Her thoughts were interrupted by a tiny squeak. Victoria jumped back. "What was that?"

Kirkpatrick grinned at her reaction. It shouted 'City-girl', she knew. "I don't know, Victoria. Let's see."

He carefully lifted the branch he had been about to hack away. A tiny tan furball with bands of white, black, and brown running down its back was trapped beneath the limb. The entire striped 'part and parcel' summed up to about three inches of squeak.

"It's a chipmunk!" Victoria beamed. She had fallen in love with the little critters ever since she had come to Kirkpatrick's woods. In the early afternoons they scampered all around the forrest floor by the cabins. They were very sweet creatures. The ones near Kirkpatrick's cabin were not timid at all.

Victoria chalked that up to the fact that he fed them peanuts every now and then.

"So it is." He ran his glove-covered finger gently over the little guy. The fur was singed in a few spots. "He's pinned by this smaller branch."

"Is he hurt?'

"Can't tell yet." He put his machete down on the ground. "If he doesn't scamper out when I lift this up he's hurt."

Kirkpatrick lifted the edge of the limb. The chipmunk tried to right himself but fell over.

Victoria's heart sank. "Oh, he is hurt! The poor thing. Can we do anything?"

"Well, that depends on what's wrong with him." He gently scooped the chipmunk up in his palm. "Looks like his rear leg is snapped."

Victoria nodded, slightly nauseous at the sight of the dangling limb.

"I have an emergency medkit back in the trailer. Do you think you can get it for me?"

"Yes, of course."

"The path we took is right through that strand of trees there." He pointed to it. "Stay on the path and don't leave it, understand? It's easy to get lost here and– On second though, I'm coming with you."

"I can go, Duncan."

"I'm coming with you." He pushed the goggles away from his face, letting them hang around his neck.

They backtracked to the trailer. When they got there, Kirkpatrick put the chipmunk gently down on the bed and grabbed the first-aid kit. Then he snapped a small twig off a nearby bush.

"What are you doing?"

"I'm going to set the leg with some tape and this twig. I don't know if he has any other injuries; he may have internal ones. If he makes it through the next few days, he might survive."

Kirkpatrick removed his gloves, getting some surgical tape and scissors out of the box. He cut the width of the tape into several narrow strips, sizing down the width as much as he could for the tiny leg.

Victoria watched him go about setting the limb. *Those large hands are so gentle.*

The chipmunk was either dazed or very ill because he didn't put up any fuss at all while Kirkpatrick went about binding his leg.

In no time, the striped guy had a tiny splint.

"Let's see what that does for him."

"What will we keep him in?"

Kirkpatrick looked around, his sights resting on the wooden tool chest in the bed of the trailer. "I'll empty that out. Should hold him fine till we get home."

He emptied the tools onto the bed and carefully placed the animal inside. But not before he took off his shirt and made a bed for the chipmunk. "I'll leave the top completely off the chest; he isn't going anywhere."

"Do you want to go back? It's starting to get chilly and all you have on is a tee shirt."

"Nah, I'll be fine. Why don't you sit and rest with Sparky here while I finish with that branch?"

"Sparky?"

He grinned. "Seems to fit. He was in that limb when it

was struck by lightening."

She rolled her eyes. *Sparky.* "Okay. I'll just sit back and enjoy the view." She lifted her brows up and down as she stared at his muscles splendidly revealed by the short-sleeved shirt.

He raised his eyebrows before turning back into the woods, disappearing quickly in the trees.

The rumble-thump of wood hitting the trailer snapped Victoria awake.

"*Whaa*???"

"Aye. Great lookout. Glad I left my most expensive tools here. Didn't you once work as a guard at the Gardener Museum in Boston?"

"Hey, what can I say? A cool breeze, warm sun, shushing tree branches, birds chirping. . . All the ingredients were there, man."

He laughed. "You know what you get when all the ingredients are there?" He held his hand out to her.

Victoria took it and jumped down from the trailer.

His caught her in his arms. Before she knew it, he dipped her, laying one arm across her back for support. His fingers delved into the hair at the nape of her neck. She clutched his shoulders for balance.

"Kirkpatrick!"

His mouth fused over hers in a curl-your-toes kiss that made her whole body sing.

Agilely, he backed her up against the trailer bed.

Victoria noted that his skin was slightly damp from the physical work he had just done; she was sorry to have missed the sight of him sawing down that tree. Kirkpatrick was good to look at; especially when he–

His jean-clad knee wedged between her thighs.

The enticing scent of cloves and musk assailed her as he kissed her senseless. His hands slid down her back, cupping her rounded buttocks. Gently clasping the globes resting in his palms, he brought her to him. Pressed her into his groin.

He was rock hard.

She stirred against his chest. Breathy. Breathless. "What-what are you doing?"

"I'm. . ." He took tiny bites along her throat and shoulders and whispered between every kiss. ". . .seeing-if-I-am-out-of-your-system-yet."

Victoria moaned as he rubbed his knee against the juncture of her thighs. Just being with him had made her wet all day.

Not a particularly good sign that she was clear of him.

She was soaking now.

He covered her mound with his hand, the heel of his palm pressing into her. Her jeans were damp right through the heavy denim. And she was so hot, in that *one* spot.

He cocked an eyebrow. "I'm guessin' the answer is no."

"Duncan, you–"

His lips covered hers; his tongue demanded entrance to her mouth.

Kirkpatrick always waited for her to make the first

move. Once she did, he exploded into sexual heat. He had never once told her he wanted her. He never once initiated lovemaking.

Until now.

How could such a passionate man stay so far away from civilization? What did he do throughout the days, months, years when he was alone?

She broke free of his lips.

His mouth scorched a trail over her cheeks, forehead, throat. "What is it?" Even as he was involved caressing her, he was attuned to her mood.

"Nothing, really. . . Well, actually there is something I was wondering about– what do you do here all the time by yourself? You don't own a television– not necessarily a bad thing, I agree– but it is a window to the world. No clubbing. No nearby restaurants. No shopping malls. The winters here are long. . ."

He seemed amused by her question. "I live, Victoria, I just live."

"But. . . I could never. . . I mean, a career is very important. If I lived in a place like this– a person like me? I would have to *do* something."

A line creased the center of his forehead. "When did it become a crime for people to simply live their lives? Why can't you just be Victoria– a person who lives. Why this compelling need to be defined by a job? Think of how ludicrous that is! You are the only person who can truly define yourself. No one will ever be able to better make the assessment of all that is you– so why box yourself into such a narrow reference?"

She crossed her arms over her chest. "Fancy talk, but what about you?"

"What about me?

"You don't just live here, as you claim. You have a lucrative, thriving career."

"No. No, I don't. People come to me for what they want and I create it. The work I do does not define me. It is the opposite– I define the work."

"You have that luxury because you have a creative gift."

"It's not a luxury; it's a necessity. I *have* to create. It's part of who I am. It may be a part of who you are, too."

"Why do you say that?"

"Why do you think?"

The front of her sneaker plowed into a small mound of dirt underfoot. Twice. "I have no idea. It sounds as if you think I should find a place and go live in the woods to do. . . what? Live off the land? I'm not that kind of person."

"I never said that. But now that you brought it up, what kind of person are you, Victoria? Maybe there is something inside of you that you can discover in these woods and take with you forever."

Maybe. She watched a few bugs scurry over the dirt she had disturbed.

His finger went under her chin and lifted her face to his. "I take a tree and see a new life for it. I fashion it into something different; its next stage of life. You can do the same."

"You want me to be a woodworker?" she remarked facetiously.

He looked at the treetops. "No. I don't think the craftsmen's guild is ready for that."

"Very funny."

He met her eyes, seriously. "Look, I want you to find the heart of yourself and fashion *that* into your journey."

250

"And what journey might that be?"

"That's not for me to say. You have to find your own kind of woods."

She rolled her eyes. "Are you serious?"

"Very."

"C'mon, KirkPatrick, you sound like some ancient Arthurian seer or a woodland. . ."

"*Druid*?" He gave her a considering look. "That was what you were going to say, wasn't it?"

"Okay, I'm sorry; but why do you even care what I do?"

"You ask me that?" He seemed wounded. "I care about all things that grow, Victoria. When you stop growing, you wait to die. Until you reclaim what is inside you, you can never have the life you want. Find what resonates within you and do it. Then come back and see me."

His words gave her pause. Maybe he was right. *Maybe*.

That didn't mean she was ready to agree with him or to stop giving him the business. "So you're the ancient custodian of our forests, the one I've heard so much about?"

"Something like that, " he said softly.

"Go know."

"It is why you came looking for me, isn't it?"

She snorted. "I never came looking for you. I just found you."

"Maybe I found you." He took her hand. "Let's find that tree."

And so he led her through his forrest.

He knew every tree, could identify every sound.

Twice, he walked her to small ponds. He knew birds by sight and by their calls. And he steered her carefully around patches of poison ivy which grew in three-leaf clusters along the vine.

Victoria realized this *was* Kirkpatrick's forrest. In every sense.

"Do you own this land?"

He gave her a mysterious smile. "You might say I'm a trustee."

Her brow furrowed. "You mean, like, for a corporation?"

"More like a conservancy. But I think what you are really asking is if I hold the deed and the answer to that is yes."

She watched him out of the corner of her eye as they walked along. There were at least five hundred acres here!

It was clear that Kirkpatrick was a naturalist; and considering his love of the land, his responses were not surprising. It was just that she had never pictured him as a land baron. Five hundred acres of prime forrest land was worth a great deal of money.

Yet he led such a simple life. . .

But wasn't it rich?

Every day brought a peaceful excitement, a serene beauty.

In the city, some days, she had to force herself to get up to face the mad rush of corporate day. Here in Kirkpatrick's woods, she woke up every morning refreshed, renewed. She wanted to capture every minute of every day.

So she took her own time to tend her plants, pick her flowers, arrange her bouquets in old bottles and buckets. The riot of hues from her plant palette seeped around the lake, turning the green and blue scenery into bursts of vivid color.

These woods made her love this life again.

Awakening to a simple concept of existence had reawakened her to the promise that life whispered when she first yearned to leave home and make her mark on the world.

"*There.*" Kirkpatrick stopped walking suddenly. "That's our tree."

He pointed to a large oak about twenty feet in front of them. One of the central branches, laden with heavy leaves, had shirred off, splitting from the main trunk. "You see that split on the main trunk?"

She nodded.

"They call this kind of branch a sucker limb. It's best if they are pruned off early. This one kept growing out– almost sideways. It became too strong, too heavy. The weight of it caused the split. You find this a lot in the birch trees around here; the limbs curve out in huge swooping arcs."

"Ah, but one could do worse than be a swinger of birch trees," she quipped.

He chuckled. "Even after first Frost?"

"Ouch," she groaned.

"So what do you think?" he gently squeezed her hand.

"About the tree?"

"Yes."

It was the first time he had asked her opinion on his work. She was no expert on wood and told him so. Still, her answer seemed very important to him.

"How can I tell?" Her hand swung in his, in a warm gesture of friendship.

He gazed softly down at her. "Just use your intuition."

Victoria cocked her head to the side and examined the tree. "Are you just going to take that sucker limb?"

He shook his head. "The whole tree. It looks fine and healthy now but by next spring rot will set in where the split occurred and it will suffer a slow, suffocating death. But if I cut it and cure the wood while it is still in the high spirit – that will make for a fine bed."

"Are you saying that the tree would approve, Kirkpatrick?" She grinned outright.

A roguish dimple curved his cheek; his brogue became thick. "Yes, it would approve and why *wouldna* it? Preserved at its peak and transformed into a cherished new form? It will bath its sleepers in the grace of its good wishes."

Victoria adored when Kirkpatrick got all Celtic on her. The mischievous way his eyes twinkled. The hint of a delicious, naughty smile.

"Well then, put that way. . ." She looped her arm through his. "I think there is no other tree but this one that will be right." She affected a brogue. "You must take this tree, Duncan Kirkpatrick, and deliver it from an unjust fate!"

"That's my way of thinking, Ms. Victoria." He clasped her wrist to hand seal the deal.

A few days later Victoria poked her head into his workshop.

After they had come back from their tree-hunting expedition, she had scurried off to her cabin, thinking that perhaps he would want to spend some time alone. After all, he was a solitary man and she had intruded on his solitude enough for that day.

Although he never made her feel that she was intruding.

Just the opposite.

He had always welcomed her.

Lately, they had been spending more time together. Most of it very heated.

For whatever reason, Victoria had come to the conclusion that Kirkpatrick needed one of the plants she had picked up at the nursery in the village. "I thought this mum would look perfect on your porch; would you like it?"

He smiles to himself. He had wondered how long it would take for the color to reach his side of the lake, to spread to his home. To enrich every aspect of his day. Soon each breath he takes will be filled with rich, new scents. . . Each glance a new texture of color. . . .

"I'd love it, thanks," he answered nonchalantly, not even looking up from the wood he was examining.

"Great."

He pointed to some drawings on his desk as he lifted a plank he had cut. "What do you think?"

Victoria put down the pot she was holding and sauntered over to the desk. A half-eaten bag of peanuts rested beside some penciled drawings. As she approached the table, a small squeak sounded.

Victoria's face lit up. "Sparky!"

The little chipmunk was corralled on top of the drawing board by a small, makeshift wooden fence. Kirkpatrick's handiwork. "He looks so much better!"

"Tell me about it. He's been criticizing everything I do. For such a little fella, he's got a lot of opinion going for himself."

Victoria laughed. "Who'd have thunk that a chipmonk would tell *you* what to do, Kirkpatrick?"

He grinned in agreement. "I thought he'd like to get out of the box. He was crawling about, dragging the splint behind him. Naggin'. Naggin'. Naggin'. So I was forced to get a little fence going for him. Now if I don't throw him a nut every ten minutes or so, he keeps squeaking until I give it to him."

"Never should have introduced him to peanuts. Looks like Sparky's imprinted on you– you know, like the ducklings do? Probably thinks you're his mom." That really deserved a smart-mouthed grin and she gave it to him.

Kirkpatrick grimaced. "You might watch that kind of talk."

She chuckled. "Well, it's obvious. Do you think he'll be okay?"

"Looks like it. Tough little guy."

As promised, the ten-minute interval of squeaking commenced. Victoria reached into the bag of peanuts and tossed Sparky one. Tiny claws immediately snatched it up.

Crunching sounds of ecstasy followed.

She lightly ran the tip of her finger over the mohawk on top of the chipmunk's head. They seemed to share a similar hairstyle. She smiled to herself. Despite his feisty attitude, he seemed very tame.

"You said you're making a bed out of the tree you cut yesterday?"

"Mmmm." Kirkpatrick spoke around a pencil in his mouth; he was picking up wood planks and alternately marking them.

Victoria noted that he had taken his shirt off. His chest and upper arms were moist with a damp sheen. The ends of his hair were wet as well; they slid against his neck and the top of his shoulders whenever he moved. Apparently he had taken a dip in the cool, clear waters of the lake not too long ago. He often liked to swim and it was an unseasonably warm September day.

His hair is getting quite long.

Victoria decided she liked it. If she stayed the winter

she would try to convince Kirkpatrick not to cut it off come spring. . .

She blinked. *What am I thinking?*

She could not possibly stay the winter. Fall was coming on fast. In another few months snow would arrive and refuse to leave until spring.

When he had first given her the use of the cabin he had mentioned that she could stay through the summer. How long would it be before she over-stayed her welcome?

She bit her lip. He had been so wonderful to her, the last thing she wanted to do was become the Guest Who Never Leaves.

"By the way, Kathy Beringer came by this morning." Kirkpatrick examined another stack of planks.

"Chit! Chit! Chit! "

Victoria tossed Sparky another peanut. *How many nuts can a chipmunk eat before it gets sick?* "Really? Did she say what she wanted?"

"She was looking for you. I told her that Ms. Victoria rarely sees the light of day before eleven." He flashed her a white-toothed, pencil-gripping grin over his shoulder.

"I am on a vacation, of sorts."

He snorted.

"I vaguely remember someone knocking on the win-dow sash, mumbling something about the garden. . .?"

He nodded sagely. "Some of us are born to see the break of day– you, Ms. Victoria, are not one of those people. You will never be one of those people."

"Hey!"

He put his hands up in a placating gesture. "But you do shine bright at night under the light of a moon." His eyes twinkled, reminding them both of that first time.

She blushed slightly. She had never been so uninhibited in her life as she had been that night. Embarrassed, she quickly changed the subject back to Kathy. "So what did she want? Did she say?"

"She was really impressed with your landscape design around the cottage."

"*Landscape design*??" Her brow furrowed. "All I did was add some color with flowering plants, and painted pots. It's just something I've always liked to do. It's no big thing."

He raised his eyebrows up and down. "Not according to her. How did she put it. . .?" He scratched his jaw. "Oh, yeah, she called you a "Monet of the Garden'."

Victoria's mouth dropped. "Really? She said that?"

"Uhuh. She said you created a magical garden. She's completely enchanted by it. She even called you a 'landscape artiste'."

"No shit?"

He grinned. "No shit."

"Wow."

"Yeah. Wow."

"And she wanted to tell me all of this and you *let* me sleep through her visit?"

"Who am I to interfere with mother nature?"

"Who indeed." She threw a peanut at him.

He tried not to smile but his lips twitched anyway. "Apparently she's opening another store. In Napa Valley, I think she said. . ."

Victoria sucked in her breath. "Napa?" She had always wondered what it would be like to live in Napa Valley. Warm, colorful, sunny. *Wineries.*

Victoria bit her lip. "Did she say anything else?"

"Let me think. . ." He rubbed his chin. The gesture was

highly overdone.

"Kirkpatrick!"

"Hmm?" But he couldn't keep the grin sneaking out of his mouth this time. "Okay. She wanted to know if you would consider going out there in October for two or three months. She wants to give the project to you and when you hear what she wants to pay you, you might even thank Roncon's greed for opening this door for you."

"This is amazing!" Her whole face lit up as she considered the possibilities.

"It is, isn't it?" Kirkpatrick watched her carefully. "This could lead to something for you– if you want it to. Other jobs, other cities. You never know. . ."

"That's right! I didn't even think of that part! I am so excited! I can't believe–" She stopped as another thought occurred to her. If she took the job, she would be leaving here within the month. *Leaving Kirkpatrick.*

She wasn't sure she was ready for that.

He watched her from under hooded lids, as if he knew what she was thinking.

Afraid he would bring it into the open, she quickly turned and examined his notes on his project. "What does quarter-sawn mean? I'm assuming it's a different way to cut the wood?"

"That it is. The growth rings of the tree are app-roximately perpendicular to the board face; normally they're cut in parallel."

"It changes the look of the wood?"

"Yeah. You take a log and cut it into quarters then each quarter is worked by taking boards from alternating faces. You end up with a plank with a concentric ring pattern."

"Okay, I know what you're talking about; this cut shows

the growth pattern of the wood." Somehow she knew that would be important to him.

"Yes."

"These drawings are beautiful, Duncan. I've always loved four-poster beds. What are these figures you've sketched on the headboard?"

He had etched a ring of women in flowing loose gowns standing around a large vat. She had seen some of his artistic carvings on other pieces he had done, but none seemed as elaborate as this design.

He came up behind her, she could feel the musky heat of him.

"They are the Nine Maidens of Celtic lore." His chin came over her shoulder, his hand came around her left side. He used the eraser tip of the pencil he was holding to tap points of the picture as he explained the scene. "The maidens breathe on the flames, keeping the cauldron hot."

"Why. . ." She felt *his* warm breath caress her neck. Keeping her hot. She cleared her throat. "Why do they do that?"

"The cauldron is the symbol of beginnings and of metamorphosis. Legends say that when we partake of these offerings from the cauldron, we feed our souls. The maidens keep the flame of life alive by blowing on it. The contents of the cauldron are ever changing, ever growing, like the land it sits upon."

"Like your woods?" She turned her head, staring straight into the forrest reflected in his eyes from the window.

"Exactly," he murmured. "You didn't come here just to give me this plant, did you?"

"No."

He viewed her askance. "If you're leaving in a month,

we're going to have to try a bit harder to get me out of your system."

"Yes, I suppose that's right." She glanced out of the window. Out to the woods surrounding them.

He dropped the pencil and brought his arm around her waist. He drew her close to him. "I have an idea that might work," he whispered into her ear.

"You do?" Her voice held the breathy quality of a person willing to try anything to solve a problem she didn't quite understand.

And that seemed to please Kirkpatrick.

He sure as hell liked being her personal problem.

"Move into the main cabin with me."

Her head whipped to him. "*What*?"

"It's the only thing I can think of." He shrugged his shoulders. "A steady diet of Kirkpatrick might do it."

Victoria chewed her lip, thinking it over. It sounded insanely reasonable. But they'd be, well, living together. Could it work?

"What do you think?" His teeth caught her earlobe in a slow, sharp tug.

Victoria shivered. "I- I think it's worth a try."

Kirkpatrick smiled against her throat. "Mmmm-hmmm."

Then he drew her into the full circle of his arms.

That afternoon he took her right there in the studio, standing up against a curved bookcase he had made.

He placed her hands high above her head as he stood behind her, his hands clasped over hers. He guided their hands along the smooth curves of the wood, then he brought their joined hands over her curves, caressing her.

He was telling her she could transform like the wood

had been transformed.

Or is he the one transforming me?

Kirkpatrick took her standing against the curved wood. Against the cusp of change. In a mellow, sensual circadian rhythm.

Victoria moved in with him that night–

But she talked him into sharing her small cabin.

Throughout September he loved in as many ways as an artist can conjure.

Victoria stood outside her cottage viewing the results of her handiwork.

The sun was setting over the western side of lake. Golden-red ribbons, the last of the day's rays, floated across the rippling water. A light breeze ruffled through the trees. . .

Shush-shush. . . Shush-shush. . . Wind brings the news. . .
The woods are most alive before winter comes. . .

The small cottage barely resembled the ramshackle cabin she had found four months ago. She had layered six colors of paint on the small house. Six colors because no human being or cabin should be forced to be just one.

Starting with Bermuda Pink as a base coat, she accented the porch, railings, window sashes and shutters with complementary tones of purple, lavender, green, periwinkle blue, and coral.

She had created a faux path to the door with a melange of potted flowering plants of roses, peonies, geraniums, sunflowers, and now-late-blooming hardy mums. She taken the plain terra-cotta pots and transformed them with paint and an eye for detail.

She had created a new, living sculpture against the canvas of a once discarded tumble-down shack.

Tomorrow she would be leaving.

Kathy Beringer had come by again and this time Victoria had been wide awake. She had listened to the woman's offer and she had accepted the opportunity.

A lump rose in her throat.

Tomorrow she would be leaving her Duncan.

Despite the fact that they had been living together for the last month, and Kirkpatrick had done his best, he was not out of her system.

All she had to do was think of the way he touched her, stroked her, and worshipped her body.

The way he sunk into her in the middle of the night over and over again.

The way he whispered her name during passages of intense connection between them, his brogue like a summer breeze lilting through the forrest.

But he never once suggested that she should not go.

When she talked about the new opportunity he watched her silently, his eyes glowing in support. He told her, "This will be a good thing for you, Victoria; you'll see. It's what you've been looking for your whole life."

He wanted her to take the chance, she knew that.

He wanted her to find her life again.

Yet the thought of leaving him weighed heavily on her. She wiped her damps hands down the front of her jeans.

Soon it would be dark.

In the past hour, thumps and clanks were issuing from the rear of the cottage. Kirkpatrick told her he had a surprise for her– for her last night.

She had duly promised not to peek.

But curiosity was getting the better of her. What was he doing in there?

"Okay, C'mon in." Kirkpatrick held the screen door open for her.

"It's about time; it's getting cold out here," she grumbled in jest. Then she crossed the porch and entered the cabin.

"Now just what was so– " She sucked in her breath. *"Oh, Duncan, it's gorgeous!"*

He had lit the logs in the stone fireplace and thrown spices on the hearth to scent the room. The glow of the fire bathed the incredible work of art dominating the room.

The bed was finished.

Four magnificent posters of quarter-sawn oak and a breathtaking, intricately carved headboard. The Maidens of Legend seemed to cast a spell over the bed as they ruled the cauldron from the headboard. Their expressive faces beckoned with a promise that those who choose to lie here will be rewarded with fresh beginnings; they will walk anew in the bounty of their good will.

In awe of his work, Victoria clasped her hands together over her chest. "Duncan. . . it's breathtaking! Your best work yet. Your client will surely treasure it."

"It's for tonight, Victoria. *For us."*

Her mouth dropped. "You created this for us? *For one night?"*

"One perfect night can live forever."

Her eyes filled with tears. "Oh, Duncan, I can't believe you did this!"

His arms came around her. "And why wouldna I?" His lips traced the nape of her neck. "Do you have any idea what you have given me?"

She brushed away a teardrop. "Um, let's see. . . I intruded into your space; I took over your spare storage area; I planted myself here for an entire season without paying rent; and I practically forced you to sleep with me. If that isn't bad enough, I refer to you sexually as some kind of infection I have to get rid of–"

His laughter interrupted her assessment.

Her mouth turned down. "Well, it's true!"

Still chuckling, he shrugged her comments off. "It's all a matter of perspective."

"Perspective?"

"Mmmmm-hmmm. And something tells me you don't quite understand mine."

Her brow furrowed. "What do you mean? Do you even have a perspective in this madness?"

"Of course I do."

"Well?" She put her hands on her hips. "What is it?"

"I think you'll figure it out on your own. I've always believed it is best when we come to our own conclusions."

"Hmph!" But she grinned. "Why do you have to always be the enigmatical wise woodsman?"

"Because that's my part."

"Oh really."

"If the chipmunk fits. . ."

"Ha!"

He took her hand and drew her to the bed.

With her hand still in his, he sat on the mattress. "C'mon, Ms. Victoria." He nodded toward the headboard. "Let's try her out and see what happens."

What did he mean by that? Victoria pulled up short. Even after all this time, Kirkpatrick was still a mystery. "Is- is something going to. . . I mean, you aren't really an ancient druid or something like that. . .?"

He gave the inscrutable Kirkpatrick gleam, which, of course, did not answer her question.

But it did turn her insides into Jell-O.

Lamentably, insides turning into Jell-O are hard to hide from a man. Especially a Scotsman.

Kirkpatrick tugged her onto the bed, rolling across the feather mattress with her. By design, he landed on top. Victoria was pinned under his tall frame.

He bent over her; the ends of his hair brushed her cheeks, silky as down.

"This is your last chance."

"For what?" She arched her eyebrows in a saucy manner. Although, she didn't think she did wench well.

His snort of incredulity confirmed it.

"You've tried a one-timer with me. Then a one-night stand." The tip of his finger traced her mutinous lower lip. "That was followed by a live-in situation. . ."

He paused dramatically.

"And?"

"And all present know what the result of that has been."

"Your point, Kirkpatrick?" Her hands massaged the back of his head, sinking into his hair. She sifted the dark honey amber between her fingers.

"My point is this is your last chance, because if you don't get me out of your system tonight– well, that could be serious."

"You think so?"

"I do." He tugged the edge of her collar back with his teeth. Warm, damp lips fastened on her throat, drawing on her flesh, tingling her to her toes.

"Wh-what will h-happen if I don't get you out of my system tonight, Duncan?"

"If that should happen, my Victoria, it may take longer than you ever thought possible."

His hands delved under the waistband of her jeans, cupping her bottom, bringing her tight against the bulge in his groin.

"How much longer?" She rubbed against him.

"It may take a lifetime." One of his hands reached around and unzipped her pants. He began tugging her jeans off.

"Really?" She lifted her hips to aid him.

Kirkpatrick hesitated for a second as if he were mulling it over. Then he swiftly pulled her panties off. "Of course I could be wrong."

He unzipped his jeans.

Victoria regarded him warily. "In what way?"

"It might take longer." Without further ado– and with an insolent Scottish grin– he thrust into her honeyed warmth.

He made love to her that night as he never had before.

As he fashioned raw wood into beauty, so too, that night, he fashioned their lovemaking into its own work of art, a profound and new entity, a creation all its own.

Once he brought the creation into being he forced her to view it.

Kirkpatrick's eyes captured hers: they spoke of legends

past, of the dimensions of the questing mind, of the wisdom of the forrest, and of the knowledge that is passed between man and woman.

If his spell wasn't magick, it was born of nature.

No less powerful. No less divine.

His touch was an ancient map, long forgotten by most men. He enveloped her in the silence of his passion. And when he rhythmically moved in her, surging back and forth, calling to her, rising, plunging, she saw the nine ancient women dancing about her, their hands joined, their hearts joyous.

The flames of change rose up, enveloping them both.

"Duncan," she cried out. "*Duncan*!"

But, as most creatures of the forrest, he was lost in the fire.

It is sometimes a necessary death.

Still, when the ashes of passion were spent, what would arise?

Victoria had no idea. It didn't matter to her. This was a journey she was taking to its completion.

When the morning came, sure of its day, clear, she knew that the road before her was about to curve.

It would do that for the rest of her life.

The curious thing was that she was glad of it. Like most, she had always assumed that her path in life was meant to be a straight line. It was what she had been taught; it was what she had believed. Progress was linear. She had never envisioned that one could actually go forward on a path that bent in on itself.

But the world is round, the universe is forever, time is transitory, and life is curved.

When she was ready to leave, he walked her out to her car. He closed the driver's side door after she got in and leaned on the open window.

She would never forget the way he looked as he told her he would miss her. He had even held Sparky up for her to kiss goodbye. Kirkpatrick had healed the chipmunk much as he had healed her.

With the glare of the morning sun behind him, he seemed to shimmer. For a second she lost sight of him.

Her hand cupped the side of his handsome face. *"Are you real, Kirkpatrick?"*

He clasped her hand and placed a kiss upon her palm. "As real as you want me to be."

"Good." Duncan was the best reflection of her hopes and dreams. He was the part of her that searched for beauty. Connection. Love. "Then this doesn't have to be goodbye."

"No. It's a fare-thee-well."

"What's the difference?"

"A fare-thee-well means I'll always be here. Waiting for you." His eyes crinkled at the corners.

Victoria laughed.

She would come back to him. Some day. Some time. Just as she knew he would welcome her.

But what if he disappeared into the woods like Brigadoon in its mists and she couldn't find her path to him?

She had to remember the way.

"How will I find you again, Kirkpatrick?"

"I'm easy to find." His finger traced the side of her face. He smiled softly. Eyes of forrest moss stared at the path in his woods. "All you have to do, Victoria, is follow that road."

He is the woods, the land, the roots. She can never get him out of her system. He is everything right and good in her life. He is the part of herself that she speaks to late at night. The part she looks for in vain during the light of day. She never wants to lose him.

He is her once and future way home, who dwells in the romance of her heart.

AUTHOR'S NOTE

Dear Readers,

In Kirkpatrick's Woods is a special work that was written specifically to honor romance readers and the heroes they love. I hope you enjoyed this different kind of story.

Whenever I travel and meet readers at booksignings, panels, airport lounges, (or the way station between Alpha Epsilon 3 and 4), the one thing I hear over and over is, "Oh, if only your heroes were real!"

Say it, sister.

At some point or other, all of us go through difficult times. During those times, it is often our beloved romance novels that help us get through painful transitions.

While going through my own 'difficult time', I asked myself: "Where do we women go when we read romance novels?"

The answer I came up with is: we go to Kirkpatrick's Woods.

The premise for this story was hatched, I then decided to play with the allegory to enrich the reader's experience. This entire tale was carefully constructed so that throughout the telling of the story we do not know if anyone but Victoria actually interacts with Duncan Kirkpatrick. Even dear Kathy Beringer is suspect as Victoria admits that she heard someone mumbling at her window.

Does Victoria find his house on the lake with the guest cabin or does she come upon a run down shack that she stays in; and bit by bit, as she heals, renovate? And why does Duncan have a surname, while Victoria doesn't? Is Kirkpatrick a druid of the forrest who opens a path for our heroine to find? Or is it *Victoria* that doesn't exist and the entire story is the mental ramblings of a hermit named Kirkpatrick who lives in the woods? "Whoa! That would be too bizarre, even for me!"

Victoria and Sparky do share a commonality (and hairstyle) in that they are both healed by Duncan Kirkpatrick; but I leave the individual reader to answer the above questions to their liking. (As a special tie-in treat, if you like, you can also come by my website www.OfficialDaraJoy.com to discuss your thoughts and let your answers be heard and registered on a poll page dedicated to this story.)

If you are of a more pragmatic ilk, you can feel free to claim that Kirkpatrick did not exist, that he was part of a troubled woman's episode as she flirted with depression and despair during a turning point in her life. You can maintain that Kirkpatrick was her vehicle back out of that road; a positive metaphor for the gift of romance novels.

If, however, you believe in quantum possibilities and the magick that love brings to healing; well, then, Kirkpatrick is as real as you could want him to be, embodied with the best of our ideals. And I will tell you that should you ever have need of this man, he will invite you to dwell in his woods. There will be a moon shining on the waters of the lake. A flickering flame in the window will cast shadows across a luxurious, intricately carved bed. Around those flames you will observe nine maidens, the muses of his circle.

Their perfect breaths will keep the cauldron of your dreams forever alive.

They speak to those who will listen–

They promise that some where, some time, some place, in some context, our heroes are most definitely real.

May you continue to have many lifetimes of joy within the pages of your books.

Love Always,
Dara

Druidsong

I am priest of the forrest
There be oak here and
There be pine
Sown in wisdom
Sown in wine
I can offer a leaf
To the forlorn
And for the sickly
A blessed acorn
I am priest of the forrest
I make your path
I sow your seeds
Here there be
Lessons of eternity
Wind is my gage
Earth is my word
Root is my sword
Branch is my sage
I am priest of the forrest
Here there be yesterday
Here there be Tomorrow
Future grows from past
Wood is arrow, wood is bow
Walk the rushes of thyme
Invite your next self
To shift into peregrine

Lift your eyes to sky
Seek, twirl, fly
When hawk becomes lion-
Then here there be dragon.
I am priest of the forrest
Learn to see my faces
Know me in bark
Know me in dark
For there be your holy places.

SPECIAL FEATURES

\\\\\\\\\\\\\\\\\\\\\\\\\\\\\

DELETED SCENES

\\\\\\\\\\\\\\\\\\\\\\\\\\\\\

Soosha's palms slid down her gown.

"My thanks to you for lending me this beautiful gown. It is very rich to the touch." She grinned at him like a cat that has found a particularly comfortable and pleasing coverlet to claim.

The reaction charmed him. "It is yours to keep."

Soosha gasped. "No, I could not!" She bit her lip then peeked up at him. "Could I?"

She was very engaging.

"Yes, you can." Daxan grinned at her, showcasing two dimples.

Of course she wanted the gown. And of course she would end up having it– all the while entrancing him as she got her way.

"Well, if I *must*." Her laugh was the kind that made one want to laugh with her.

Her laughter almost made him *beg* to know her.

He was wearing a sleeveless white tunic that was belted snugly at his waist.

His feet were bare.

Most Spoltami men dressed in such a way. It seemed most comfortable. For some reason it reminded Soosha of lazy days spent stretching contentedly in the sun.

His golden skin made the contrast *purr-able*.

Daxan Sahain had a quality she had seen in but a few men. She always called it "the warm, stroking touch". When she looked at a man like him, she wanted to go into his arms and feel them come about her. A sultry warmth that would comfort and arouse always went with such a touch.

It was unfortunate for this Spoltam man that female Familiars loved to tease– because Soosha saw no reason to change her behavior.

In fact there might be the thrill of danger in teasing.

Reason enough for her.

When a male challenged her, Soosha considered it an invitation to go ahead and 'try it'. Familiar's often made turnabout decisions; especially at times when others would never act in such a manner. Generally speaking, Familiar behavior was impossible to predict.

In addition to this, they were highly skilled at interpreting their opponents.

It surprised Soosha that this Spoltam male's reactions were so difficult to decipher. He was a worthy match.

Daxan walked out ot the balcony.

Leaning on the railing, he scrutinized at the city below. For an instant, Soosha sensed that he viewed the city like a man wanting out. His eyelids were half-closed and there was a dissatisfied look on his face.

As if he were forced to wait upon a particularly slow-moving prey.

Why would he feel that way about his own people?

Mayhap he did not approve of the Spoltam ways as much as he wanted her to believe?

"All of Aghni is at your feet, my lady Familiar." His tone was droll. "You should come outside and get a better view of it."

"Are you not concerned your neighbors will see a strange woman in your home?"

He gave her a slanted look. The edges of his lips curled. "That would not be such an unusual occurrence," he assured her.

Soosha arched her brows. At least he was honest. "I see."

She joined him on the balcony, standing beside him at the railing.

Familiar males generally loved to bite, although, a few preferred licking.

Some favored both.

In the throes of passion, her mate was partial to sliding his chin against her cheek in a nudge-caress. And he was definitely a biter.

Mastering of the Familiar love bite was considered an art form.

There were countless techniques and styles; all designed for one purpose– to bring forth the highest peaks of pleasure. The ancient skill had few "regal masters".

There were rumors that her brother, Brygar, was one of those elite masters, endowed with a legendary skill for the sensual bite. At least, that is what she had once overheard from a group of gossiping females attending the same festival as her.

But women had always said strange things about her

brother. One had even claimed that he became as addictive as spun honey.

Her brother?

If these women saw his impossible, stubborn male/cat ways, they would think differently!

Yaniff had the Sight.

There were those in the chamber who wondered what level of Sight he had actually attained.

\\\\\\\\\\\\\\\\\\\\\\\\\

LETTERS FROM YOU

\\\\\\\\\\\\\\\\\\\\\\\\\

I am very fortunate in that I receive a lot of response from my readers. Many a day, when I needed it the most, one of your letters would come to me and I really want to thank you all for that. Although it is impossible for me to respond to the thousands of letters I receive, I do find the time to read each and every one. I thought it would be nice to share some of these wonderful letters from around the world. The world of books crosses over all boundaries and borders and readers worldwide are members of the same family.

LETTERS FROM AROUND THE WORLD.

Centuries ago after the meal was finished The Storytellers would begin their fables and the Storyteller with the best would be well rewarded and their name would be recounted, remembered and past to others and their fame would grow. You are our Storyteller. Your tales are remembered, recounted and passed on to others and you have grown in our hearts, our minds and your stories have grown in our fantasies. I wish you the best in your battle and hope that you come out victorious. I ordered you new book and am patiently awaiting any news or updates.
Smiles,
Connie Stokes
Ellijay, GA USA

In memory of Angelia, my wife of 21 years and lover of

books. Dara Joy's books gave her a smile when she needed it most.
Charles Pfeifer
USA

[Your] books bring me such joy! I can never read them too many times. I always laugh and enjoy them, no matter how much I've read them before. If [you] wrote the NYC Yellow Pages, I'd camp out in front of the phone company for a month to be the first to get a copy!
Kati Gallarini
Kings Mountain, NC USA

Over the last year I have stumbled over a few excellent authors (only 3). Of Dara Joy's books I have accumulated quite a few. She is one of those authors who you can never put down until you have come to the end of her stories.
Bernadette
Norwich, England

Hello! How do you do? I'm your fan from Tokyo, Japan. I always enjoy your stories!
<G> Good luck!
My best wishes.
Mizuho Yoshida
Japan

I have and read many times over, Knight of a Trillion

Stars, Rejar, and Mine to Take. I need more stories...
Tonya Boyd
Okinawa, Japan

I'm a book fanatic, esp. for fiction. I've been hooked to DJ ever since Lorgin murdered the microwave.
Christie Ang
Malaysia

I love every single one of your books. . . and amid all the stress I just lock myself up with one of your books - its a real pick-me-up. I hope there are more books in the making as I type as I know I can't wait for the next one.
Anusha
Kuala Lumpur, Malaysia

I love all of your books! Can't wait for the next one!
With love from Israel!
Liat Pakter
Jerusalem, Israel

We all appreciate what you're doing. Even though the load is heavy, hang in there. Thanks a bunch.
Sana Husseini
Jordan

Love your books, hope you can continue to publish them

soon. Good luck!!
Susana
Santo Domingo, DOMINICAN REPUBLIC

Seriously speaking, I do not really have any favorite book of Dara Joy's, all her books are fantastic & I love all of them very much.... her stories are what any girl would dream/wish & more....
Vanessa Joseph
Singapore

I love Dara Joy's books and I'm hooked. I always look out for new books from Dara Joy at the bookstores. I enjoy her stories immensely and read it cover to cover.
liza
Singapore

I have totally fallen in love with Dara Joy's Matrix of Destiny books!
Therese Akerberg
Karlshamn, Sweden

I love your books. I have just recently discovered them, but I can see that I am hooked. Can't wait to read another one of your books.
Jo-ann Hew
The Netherlands

Dara Joy is the best! Her books are so very good!! Especially Matrix of Destiny books are truly magical, I LOVE THEM!! Thank you Ms. Joy for writing so wonderful books!

Terhi Spackstein
Espoo, Finland

My first introduction to a Dara Joy book was Knight of a Trillion Stars. I read it in one sitting the first time and have been an avid, yet impatient, fan ever since. As it is quite difficult to obtain certain books in South Africa, I literally hounded all the shops in all the towns I happened to be in to get my greedy little paws on Rejar. I'm happy to say that I finally tracked one down and immediately bought it without even glancing at the price. I am yet again reading the three books in the Matrix series and am impatiently waiting for the story about Traed. If I didn't know any better, I would definitely say that I am your biggest fan, but I know that my friend is also one of your followers. In fact, between the two of us I am the only one who has Rejar and we frequently swop it around - I think we are going to read it to pieces. Thank you for sharing your wonderful heroes with us.

Jackie Godfrey
South Africa

This book was absolutely fabulous. Thank you Dara Joy!! Don't ever stop writing.

Ursula Dawn Vermeulen

South Africa

Thanks for all the hours of fun that you gave me. I am a single mom with 2 boys and I usually have to wait until they are sleeping before I can really enjoy your stories. Needless to say, I see the sun come up more than once still reading your book. Can't wait for any new books from you, they are quite hard to come by in South Africa. Usually you can find any other writer in the second hand book stores, but believe you me, your books they keep. Thanks again and pleeeaaase keep up the good work on keeping us all believing that happy endings may just wait for us as well.
Raven
Mosselbay, South Africa

My aunt was the first person who introduced me to these wonderful books. She said "I'm reading this great book, where people turn into cats and this old, mischievous wizard." She left for Ireland 2 yrs ago and since then I've been searching 4 all the books, finally at a sale I found 3 (Knight of a Trillion Stars, Mine to take and Tonight or Never) Of course I cant find Rejar. These are definitely my FAVORITE books. I have read them soooo many times, I still laugh at the same things over and over again!! "We are weechukchuking!!" I love that. Dara has the most wonderful imagination, I sometimes wish my cat (Hobo) would turn into Rejar. I'd be a very VERY happy female!! Thank you so Much Dara, u make an incredibly horrible day into a sensual dream!
Luna_Angelet

Johannesburg, South Africa

I have thoroughly enjoyed all your books.
Sian Willard
Britain/Wales

Thoroughly enjoyed the 4 books I have read. I bought them "on spec" and then have read them all in a couple of days, I could not put them down, and when one was finished HAD to read the others. Brilliant. More please.
Ursula Davidson
Lucan, Ireland
I have just discovered Dara Joy and read High Energy which [was] brilliant, I have also ordered Knight of a Trillion Stars and can't wait to get my hands on it.
Mary Buckley
Dublin, Ireland

Hi Dara, I absolutely love your books, they are sexy, sensual, funny and HOT, I have read many romances but your books are the BEST and I have reread them many times, I love you, take care.
Anuradha Agarwal
Kolkata, West Bengal India

Dara,
I am truly a fanatic for fantasy books and wish there were more I could devour ;) Keep up the amazing work!

Mahaira
P.S Please add me to your mailing list if you have one.
Mahaira
Karachi, Pakistan

We are waiting very patiently for the new book, but we would like to extend further support from Australia and say we enjoy your books very much and we hope to see good things come about soon.
Well done
Rosemary Potter
Brisbane, Australia

There are very few romance authors out there that I enjoy. Dara Joy is one of my favorites though. I tend to stick with authors and will re-read over and over again the books I love.
Thank you for your great stories Dara.
Barbara Kelly
Australia

I love your books Ms Joy. They take me to a grand adventure. Please never
stop writing:-)
Linda
Australia

I've just finished reading all of your books, and I've loved

all of them. Please go on writing, I'll pray so you can be back greater than before. Thank you for all the wonderful hours you've given me through yours books.
(Sorry about the errors in the message, I'm Spanish and English is not my mother tongue)
Lupe
Spain

I love all of your books, and I search it from Spain. Thank you for your stories.
Sonsoles Herrero-Minguez
Madrid, Spain

Anyway I wanted to thank you for many things : first for the laughter you bring me every time I read your books (17th time for koats etc...) and second for the strength to give writing a try myself!
So thank you and good luck from a french girl that supports you 300 per cent!
With all my admiration and my friendship!
Katel
Saint Pierre du Perray, France

Stay who you are and never change for anyone!! Thanks for giving us these fantastic stories.
Soraya
Paris, France

Dara,
We absolutely love your work. . . If there is a way to help you tell us
big huggles
Katrin Kreizel
Paris, France

I can hardly wait to read Dara Joy's new book--finally the wait is over! I just hope this new book will be able to satisfy my insatiable desire for something--familiar!
pat alexander
Germany

I'd like to read all your books, but unfortunately, there are only 2 books in russian.
Natalia
Khabarovsk, Russia

Keep it up Dara - I'm sure lots of people like me are always breathless awaiting your next book!!!
Frances Catherine Farrugia
Mqabba, Malta

EXHILARATING AND UNFORGETTABLE BOOK
Tevita Keaw
Bangkok, Thailand

Happy New Year to you, Dara. Always waiting for your new book... I love them all.
sunan
Thailand

hi!! I am your fan
jin hee
Pusan, Korea

Hello. I really enjoyed your book yesterday. Thank you your nice books :D *sorry I am not good at English.. and I can't sure Traed's spelling, but you would know ;) Have a nice day. :D
Hana
Seoul, Korea

I especially like the Dara Joy books about other worlds. These books reveal the worlds that at the same time are known and strange. I eagerly await the book about the first warrior-woman :)
Karolina Krisciukaityte
Vilnius, Lithuania

Dara
Have never written to an author before but I've checked your website a few times hoping to hear about upcoming novels as I've loved your books and reread them again and again...

Regards
Sue Vincent
Auckland, New Zealand

I love that you allow your female characters to be strong,
but still compliment the strength of your male characters -
and that they overcome their differences to communicate
with each other - plus they have fun
sexually!
Elizabeth Farley
Auckland, New Zealand

Love your books and I have all that I can my hands on, it's a
bit hard to get all your books here as the books coming out
dates are different. I enjoyed RITUAL OF PROOF a really
different view of the world if females were to lead...
Misty
Auckland, New Zealand

Loved Ritual of Proof. When is the sequel coming out???
Lillian Holm
Hornslet, Denmark

I absolutely adore your books...
Mia1977
Austria

very very exciting!
shaira
Nairobi, Kenya

I just love her books!!!
Sarah Oyungu
Nairobi, Kenya

I love all of your books, can't wait for the rest
Jackie Milo
St. George's, Grenada

My sisters, cousins and myself are great fans of Ms Joy's work, we've got most of her books. Ms joy, if you're reading this we would like you to know that we were sorry to hear about the horrible battle going on behind the scenes, but know that you've got the most loyal and staunchest supporters in all of us, your fans. (Just say the word and we'll don our armors, raise our 'swords' and 'unleash hell'.) Anyway, like your heroes/heroines you showed the great strength of your character when you didn't (and would not) compromise your principles or your work for the 'powers that be'! So continue to dish out your masterpieces at your own rate and we will continue to await the pleasures of your talent.
nals
Trinidad & Tobago

I love your books; I can never put them down. I look forward to reading the
rest of them!
Jennifer
Vancouver, Canada

I think Ms. Joy is a wonderful author - her writing really grips you and doesn't let go - [her] characters are so engaging, it makes you wish they were real.
Kim Lovely
Regina, Canada

I have only read Dara's books in the past 2 yrs and got hooked on them. . . I also send my condolences as I lost my dad in 3/2000 from a fall in the tub too. I want to congratulate and send hand shakes to the designer of this site. It has been a pleasurable adventure and experience clicking my way through each topic and archive. Keep up the great work and I shall be returning soon I know. Thank you.
Cheryl Patykewich
Ontario, Canada

Keep writing even if I have to pay more and buy your books online, I will. Do what you need to survive and to stay true to yourself that's all I can ask as a fan. Thank you for the adventure, fun, laughs and romance that you have given me.
Michelle Waskowic

Melfort, Canada

Thank you for the gift of your talent.
linda Copeland
LINDA COPELAND
Ontario, canada

I thoroughly enjoy the books that I have read by Dara, and I look forward to many more. I just wish I could live in "My Father's Mansion."
Karen Kruger
Yellowknife, Canada

. . . The mightiest weapon lies in the hands of the masses.
Dee Mack
Mississauga ON Canada

Hi Dara,
  I think you know all of your many fans are rooting for you!!
CharlotteZimmerman
USA

I first found your works 8 yrs ago. I was going through a terrible time after the loss of my beautiful daughter. Your books gave me much laughter and heartfelt warmth. You even posted my letter on your web site for a couple of years. It was my greatest honor!!!! I haven't written in a few

years as you became so popular that I just trailed along happy for you. Merry Christmas and have a beautiful new year. Your loyal follower.. Jodie's mother.
Christeena Darden
Idabel, OK USA

I love your attention to detail and ability to make a fantasy world become totally real. There are a lot of loose ends that need to be tied up, and I can't wait for the book(s) that will do that. I also loved ROP. I think it would be a great text book for a college gender studies class. I look forward to reading your newest effort.
Pamela Keith
Washington, DC USA

Special thanks to Cory and Chris Smiley, Tavern Keeper extraordinaire and all of the "Mod Squaders" who bring so much fun and excitement to the Fanspeak and RPG Tavern Board. The best people to hang out with in any universe!

About the Author

Inside the book industry and to her countless readers worldwide, Ms Joy is considered a publishing phenomenon. Hailed as "a break-out talent" by Publisher's Weekly, blazing new trails is a top priority for this writer who especially loves to push the boundaries of fiction. She has written eight consecutive New York Times and USAToday bestselling novels. Never content to rest on her past success, Dara is a writer that takes risks.

Dara has been inducted into the Romance Writers of America "Honor roll", an exclusive list which honors top authors in the romance field. She is an active member of the Science Fiction Writers of America, as well as the Author's Guild. All of Ms Joy's novels and anthologies are still in print an amazing nine years after publication and are constantly reprinted and stay shelved at all major book chains. Her books are sold worldwide and have been translated into several languages, including German, Norwegian, Chinese, Korean, and Russian.

Come to the castle and enter the worlds of Dara
Joy on the worldwide web!
Go to: www.OfficialDaraJoy.com

Notes